MABRY'S CHALLENGE

Mabry's Challenge

Ben Tyler

FIVE STAR
A part of Gale, Cengage Learning

GALE
CENGAGE Learning·

Farmington Hills, Mich • San Francisco • New York • Waterville, Maine
Meriden, Conn • Mason, Ohio • Chicago

LIBRARY OF CONGRESS CATALOGING-IN-PUBLICATION DATA

Names: Tyler, Ben.
Title: Mabry's challenge / Ben Tyler.
Description: First edition. | Waterville, Maine : Five Star, a part of Cengage Learning, Inc. 2016.
Identifiers: LCCN 2016024390 | ISBN 9781432832896 (hardcover) | ISBN 1432832891 (hardcover) | ISBN 9781432832865 (ebook) | ISBN 1432832867 (ebook) ISBN 9781432833473 (ebook) | ISBN 1432833472 (ebook)
Subjects: LCSH: Texas Rangers—Fiction. | Murder—Investigation—Fiction. | Outlaws—Fiction. | GSAFD: Western stories. | Adventure fiction.
Classification: LCC PS3620.Y58 M33 2016 | DDC 813/.6—dc23
LC record available at https://lccn.loc.gov/2016024390

First Edition. First Printing: December 2016
Find us on Facebook– https://www.facebook.com/FiveStarCengage
Visit our website– http://www.gale.cengage.com/fivestar/
Contact Five Star™ Publishing at FiveStar@cengage.com

Printed in the United States of America
1 2 3 4 5 6 7 20 19 18 17 16

This book is dedicated to Betty, Barry, Brad, Margie, Marley, Aldyn, Katherine, and Lilly.

CHAPTER ONE

Oklahoma Territory
Spring, 1881

Deputy U.S. Marshal Frank Mabry dropped down behind an oak tree a hundred yards in front of the Tonkawa's saloon. And it was a stretch to call the leaning, weather-warped building a saloon. It wasn't much larger than the smokehouse back at Mabry's Texas panhandle ranch. How the building had withstood the Oklahoma winds this long was a mystery to him.

"What do you think, Jack?" Mabry whispered.

Jack Little Lamb held up three fingers, then pointed toward the rear of the building. "Three horses in shed behind saloon. Belong to Ryan and Ogdens."

Two more horses stood out front where they'd been loosely tied to a hitching rail. That put at least five people inside—just enough to crowd the tiny saloon. For all Mabry knew, the two horses' riders might be kinsfolk of the Ogden twins, which would complicate things further. The Ogden clan was a breed of people Mabry didn't want to go around antagonizing.

Mabry and his Cherokee tracker, Jack Little Lamb, had followed Ryan and the Ogden twins to the shack where the two lawmen now tried to determine their next move. The little Irishman, Timothy Ryan, had been known to travel with the brawny Ogden twins, Eli and Emmitt, for his protection when he'd made a big haul. Ryan had taken seventy-five thousand dollars from the Wells Fargo safe in Fort Worth, so Mabry had

7

anticipated the Irishman would meet up with Eli and Emmitt somewhere outside of Fort Worth.

They had pursued Ryan for a full day before Little Lamb found the spot where the three men had joined up. Mabry later got the break he needed near the Texas-Oklahoma Territory border where the twins had raised a ruckus in a backstreet saloon. Eli had shot a man and left him on the floor bleeding, but alive. From there, staying on their trail was a hit and miss proposition. The Ogden twins knew every back road and trail in the territory—and had traveled most of them at one time or another to elude the law.

Little Lamb had run across their trail again on the afternoon of the third day, then lost it for a spell. He found their tracks an hour later, which eventually led them to the Tonkawa's saloon.

"How we take them?" Little Lamb asked.

Mabry could tell that Little Lamb wasn't itching to tangle with the twins. He didn't disagree with the Cherokee's sentiments. The twins would as soon shoot you as not. Eli in particular. Emmitt was a little more cautious, but still dangerous with a six-shooter in his hand. To make matters worse, the twins had made it clear to anyone who'd listen they would never be put behind bars again.

Mabry was especially troubled about their brags since he had already put the two of them in jail twice. During his twenty years of law experience, he had found the third time was not always a charm.

"I don't see any way to get at Ryan without going through Eli and Emmitt," Mabry said. He thought about it for a few more minutes, then asked, "Did you see a back door to the saloon when you checked on the horses?"

Little Lamb nodded. "There is back door."

"We'll do this, then," Mabry said, pointing toward the rear of the shack. "You go around to the back door and be ready to come in when you hear a commotion inside. I'll go in the front. We might as well get on with it. We can't sit out here all afternoon and worry it to death."

Mabry waited until Little Lamb had disappeared around the corner, then pushed through the front door. Eli had his back to the door, standing in front of a wood plank that sat across two sawhorses and served as the bar. Emmitt and Timothy Ryan sat at a table off to his right with another man Mabry didn't know. The fifth man was the bartender.

Eli turned at the sound of the door opening and saw Mabry. Eli wasted no time in showing his intentions; he went for his gun and got off a wild shot before he collapsed to the sawdust floor with Mabry's bullet in his right shoulder. Mabry swung his Colt over toward Emmitt, who had flipped the table over and tried to hide behind it.

"Don't shoot, Mabry. Don't shoot," screamed Timothy Ryan, who was cowering on the floor beside Emmitt.

Little Lamb burst through the back door at the sound of the first shot and had his rifle trained on Emmitt. The man who had been sitting at the table with Ryan and Emmitt had crawled to the door in the confusion and had run away. The bartender was still on the floor where he had dropped when he saw Eli go for his gun.

"You got me, Mabry," Ryan said. "Don't shoot. I'll go with you."

Little Lamb rounded up all the guns and put them in an old flour sack he'd found behind the bar. He tied the sack in a knot and threw it over near the rear door.

"Emmitt, get over there and check on your brother," Mabry said. "See if you can plug up that hole in his shoulder and stop the bleeding."

Eli, his face pale, sat up and propped himself against one of the sawhorses. He had his left hand pressed hard against his shoulder. "I shoulda got you that time, Mabry. I beat you to the draw. I just got excited and shot too quick."

Mabry turned to Little Lamb and said, "Get Ryan tied on a horse while I tend to the twins. I want to be gone from here before any of their angry kinfolks show up." He knelt down beside Eli and checked his wound. "You should've known better than get mixed up with Ryan again, Eli." He stood, motioned toward Emmitt, and said, "Empty your pockets, boys."

"What for?" Emmitt asked. "You gonna rob us?"

"I'm sure you weren't riding along with Ryan because you like his company. Empty your pockets like I said."

The twins dumped everything they had on the floor. Mabry counted four thousand, three hundred dollars among the matches, poker chips, pocket knives, and other assorted junk.

"Looks like Ryan pays well."

"We're what you might call 'specialists' in our field," Emmitt said.

Mabry shook his head as he collected the money and stuck it in a leather bag. "You're getting off lucky this time, boys. I don't have time to deal with you like I should. I'd advise you to stay out of Texas for a few months. The next badge you run into might not be so forgiving."

"You mean you ain't taking us in?"

"Nope. But if I were you, I'd find Eli a doctor before blood poisoning sets in. Remember what I said about staying out of Texas. And it might be a good idea if you boys learned another specialty. You're not very good at this one."

"I still say I beat you," Eli said—right before he passed out.

CHAPTER TWO

Frank Mabry rode into the outskirts of the small Texas town an hour after sundown. He slowed and gazed at a splintered piece of lumber nailed to an oak tree: *Split Rock Pop 482.* Mabry had noticed a gathering of dark clouds off to the northwest and felt the wind pick up. He was certain a spring storm was in the offing, so it was time for him to find a place to hunker down for the night.

He was weary from the Timothy Ryan chase but knew the end was in sight—at least for a few days. He was two days' travel, maybe a little more, from the ranch he co-owned with his younger brother, Woodrow, near Adairsville. Now that he had caught up with Ryan, Mabry intended to take a few days off to help Woody around the spread.

Was he looking for a change in his life? Mabry had asked himself that question often during the past couple of years. Up to this point, he had lived with a gun in his hand while sitting astraddle a horse. It seemed he was eternally chasing Indians, border bandits, or common little thieves like Timothy Ryan. He scratched at his stubble and thought: I'm forty-two years of age now. Maybe it's time to start thinking of a calmer, more peaceful way of life for the future.

He'd once laughed at old-timers who had told him being a lawman got tougher as you got older. He now believed every word they had said. Mabry felt a wave of guilt sweep over him as he thought of his and Woody's ranch. Addie had so often asked him when? When are you going to quit chasing outlaws? When are you going to settle down to a normal life? When can I stop worrying about whether you're going to come back or not?

As time passed, Mabry realized that he and Addie didn't have the same dream about their future. When Addie had asked him to settle down, she hadn't meant settle down on a cattle ranch. She had Denver in mind. Or maybe Kansas City. He'd even heard her talk about living in San Francisco a few times. But live on a cattle ranch in Texas? No, thanks. He had often thanked his lucky stars he'd never taken the matrimonial step with her, as much as he had cared for her. That loop around his neck would've been chafing before the preacher had finished listening to their vows.

As he entered the outskirts of Split Rock, Mabry spotted a barn-like structure off to his left that had a weather-faded sign above its double doors: *Jake's Livery and Feed.* Mabry dismounted in front of the barn, stretched his arms over his head, and then bent over at the waist. He heard his shoulder joints crack and felt his back muscles strain at the movement. Being in the saddle all day played hell on his stocky, muscular body.

"Hey, the barn," he shouted, as he slapped his black hat at his gray shirt and frayed jeans. "Anybody about?"

A youngster of maybe twelve years came out of the barn carrying a water bucket.

Mabry reached over and tousled the boy's yellow hair. "I've been riding hard for a few days and need a bit of rest. Can you take care of my horse tonight?"

"Yes, sir. For fifty cents, I can feed him, rub him down, and put him in a stall all by hisself."

Mabry dug a few coins out of his shirt pocket and handed them to the youngster. "Here's a dollar. How about treating 'ole Moses real special tonight. He deserves it. I expect to be pulling out at first light."

"Gosh, mister. Thanks. I'll take the goodest care of him he's ever had."

Mabry smiled at the boy's excitement, then asked, "Is there a telegraph office in town?"

The youngster pointed across the street. "The Western Union office is down that way a piece. It might be open, might not be."

"How about a hotel?"

"Nope. Ain't got no hotel in town. You can bed down up in the hayloft if'n you agree not to smoke."

The first thing he needed to do would be to let his boss, Marshal Reed Bannister, know he'd caught up with Timothy Ryan. After that, he would find himself a hot meal and then make himself comfortable in the hayloft. He'd bedded down in worse places. He tugged at the Colt .45 belted around his waist, then shucked the Winchester from the leather scabbard.

"I'll leave my gear over in the corner," he said to the boy. "How about you keeping an eye on it for me?"

"I'll do that, mister. Don't you worry none."

When he reached the Western Union office, Mabry noticed a lantern glowing inside. He flipped the latch and found a balding man wearing thick eyeglasses sitting behind the customer counter reading a dime novel. The cover on the book portrayed a tall, good-looking yellow-haired man dressed in buckskins fighting off a horde of tomahawk-wielding Indians. The Indians had him encircled. Things looked dire. But the yellow-haired man had two smoking guns in his hands.

Mabry hadn't read the book, but he was pretty sure he knew how it would end.

The man looked up when the door opened. "Howdy," he said. "Can I help you?"

"I need to send a message to Dallas."

The man shoved a sheet of paper and a pencil across the

counter toward him. "You write it, I'll send it. It'll cost you six bits."

Mabry began scribbling out his message. He told Bannister he had apprehended Timothy Ryan, and that Jack Little Lamb would be delivering Ryan and the Wells Fargo money to the Fort Worth authorities. Mabry finished the message by informing Bannister that he was on his way to his Adairsville ranch. He handed his message and six bits to the telegraph operator.

At the door on his way out, he asked. "Is there a place close by where I can get a hot meal?"

"Miss Minnie's café is a couple doors down. She's an old widow woman and doesn't keep regular hours. She just closes the door when she gets tired."

"My kinda woman," Mabry said with a grin.

Mabry was lucky, as he found Miss Minnie's open for business. He'd already put away a thick, well-done steak and a piece of Miss Minnie's apple pie when the Western Union operator found him. He'd been debating the idea of ordering a second piece of pie when he was interrupted by the messenger.

"You got a message from Dallas, Mr. Mabry. I'm glad I caught you."

"Yeah," Mabry replied with a scowl on his face. "Thanks for being so conscientious."

Mabry handed the messenger two bits. He was surprised that Bannister had replied to his message. His boss was seldom in town, and even less likely to be at the office if he was in town. He read the message.

Meet me in Dallas. Cattleman's Hotel. Wed night or Thurs morn.
Room Reserved. Do not tarry. Important.

Bannister.

"Dammit," Mabry said, as he wadded up the telegram and threw it at the window. He leaned back in the chair and massaged his temples. A side trip back to Dallas would add at least three days to his travel, maybe more. It had been more than a month since he'd seen Bannister, but the tone of the message didn't bode well. It appeared he was going to have to forego his trip to his ranch and head for Dallas. Maybe it wasn't in the cards for him to become a rancher.

CHAPTER THREE

Mabry climbed down the ladder from the hayloft at first light. The rainstorm had hit during the night as he had expected. It woke him sometime during the early morning hours when he'd felt the barn shake as a stiff wind hammered against it. He had listened as the rain pelted the tin roof and the thunder rumbled. With all that, the storm failed to keep his weary body awake for more than a few minutes.

He found a wooden tub of rainwater in front of the stable and splashed a double-handful of cold water on his face. He combed his fingers through his longish brown hair, pulled out a few stems of hay, and untangled it as much as he could. Afterwards, he shook his head like a mongrel pup to get rid of the excess water.

While he saddled Moses, he thought about the ranch he and Woody had dubbed the Double-M. He'd always wondered if he was cut out to be a full-fledged rancher. He'd never even been a ranch hand, although he had always wanted to give it a try. When they decided to buy the small spread, both of them realized that Woody would carry the bulk of the work. Woody had been a freight hauler for several years and was eager to settle down to something permanent. Woody had said he didn't mind Frank being away so much since he had his wife, Stella, to keep him company, along with two ranch hands.

Frank had told his brother at the very beginning that he didn't want to quit his job as a marshal. He still relished the hunt and the challenge of trying to outthink the lawbreakers he pursued. Nor did he want to give up his regular government pay until he had a feel for how the ranch's finances would shake out. It could be the two of them were in over their heads. Looking back, he reckoned Woody and Stella had done a creditable job with the ranch during the first two years. They'd been able to pay all their bills and keep the two hands on board. Mabry had even managed to put away a few dollars in the Adairsville Bank. Still, the idea of changing careers had been creeping into his thoughts more and more of late.

The sky had cleared by morning. Mabry rounded up a bait of oats for Moses, then took to the road out of Split Rock as the sun peeked over the horizon. The travel was steady, uneventful, and tiring. He saw a few weary travelers along the way. Two men on horseback nodded at him as they passed, and a four-wagon caravan of homesteaders trudged along on the muddy road. Three young boys walked behind the caravan urging half a dozen scrawny cows to keep up with the wagons. They were most likely looking for a place to make a home in this wide open country.

By late evening, Mabry was ready to call it quits for the day. If he stopped now, he was certain he could get to Dallas by the following afternoon. He kept a sharp eye out for a favorable place to toss his blanket for the night. Right at dusk, he spotted a grove of willow trees a hundred or so yards off the road that looked promising. He supposed there would be water close by if there were willow trees growing there. Nudging Moses in that direction, he found a narrow creek running bank-full due to the recent rainstorm. He scouted around and located a high creek bank that appeared to be dry enough for an overnight camp.

He scavenged around and rounded up an armload of twigs he found under the root wad of a fallen cottonwood. Once he had a fire going, he put his coffee makings together and hung the fire-blistered enamel pot above the flames. He opened a can of beans, which he placed on a rock near the fire to warm. His supper wouldn't match Miss Minnie's steak and apple pie, but it would have to do. While supper was in the making, he moved Moses over to a grassy spot close to the creek and picketed him for the night.

Mabry ate his fill of beans, then put away a can of peaches for dessert. He crushed the empty cans and put them in his saddlebags. He then took off his black cowhide vest and his boots, but remained clothed in his shirt and denims. The sky was clear and star-filled. The storm had passed through and had left the air cooler, with a nice breeze rattling through the trees. Mabry spread out his blanket and eased himself down. He placed his revolver next to his right hand, and his rifle next to his left hand. Just in case.

He yawned as he thought about the ranch, marshaling, Addie, and a hundred other things until it was time to get serious about sleep. His eyes had begun to get heavy when he heard the first gunshot. He grabbed his revolver and boots, then rolled over into the shadows. He listened and waited. After two minutes of quiet, he pulled on his boots. Then he heard another gunshot. Not close. He cocked his head. He soon heard hoofs pounding on the road headed in his direction. Then more shots. Mabry crawled over to his blanket and took a minute to strap on his gun belt. He picked up his rifle and moved farther back into the trees, where he crouched down behind a rotting cotton-wood stump.

Soon, in the light of the quarter moon, he saw the shadowy outline of a man running on foot toward the grove of trees. The man stumbled, got to his feet, and started running again. Three riders were not far behind him, shouting and shooting.

"There he goes. Over there in the trees," one of them yelled.

The pursuers had seen the runner, too, and were closing in on him.

"Don't let him get away, Scruggs. We'll hang him right here. This is as good a place as any to string him up."

When the three riders got closer, Mabry could see they were tough-looking men with rifles in their hands. He doubted they were men of the law if they were talking about a lynching. Deputy Marshal Mabry had no use for men who took the law into their own hands. He raised up on one knee with his rifle at the ready and waited. Then Mabry saw the stranger they were chasing appear at the edge of the trees. The stranger was coming toward him. He must've seen the low-burning campfire.

"Get down quick," Mabry said. "Before they see you."

The stranger bent low as he ran over to the stump where Mabry had positioned himself. "I bring you trouble, *señor.* These men, they want to kill me."

The pursuer closest to the camp shouted, "There's a horse over here, Riker."

"Stay close. Don't let the Mexican get to it."

"I see a campfire," shouted another one.

Mabry heard the horses' heavy breathing as the men walked them toward his camp. He waited, prepared for whatever might happen next.

"Camp," one of the men shouted. "We're coming in. Don't shoot."

Mabry tossed the stranger his rifle and said, "Get behind that tree and keep quiet. No shooting unless I start it, you hear?"

"*Si, señor.* I hear."

Mabry dropped his revolver into his holster and stepped out where he could be seen. "Come on in," he said. "But I heard shots fired, so you best be moving slow and easy like."

CHAPTER FOUR

The three men rode in and stopped in front of Mabry. His first impression was right on target. They were as shabby and down at the heels a bunch as he'd ever seen. And there was not a badge among them. Then he looked down and saw that he didn't have a badge on either. It was on his vest over by the blanket.

The man on the left seemed to be the head honcho. He dismounted and walked toward Mabry. He was a broad-chested man who wore a battered hat pulled low. He had on a pair of oversized trousers that dragged the ground when he walked. His face was round and covered with a greasy beard. There was nothing pleasant looking about him.

The man pointed toward the trees with his rifle. "That Mexican we're chasing after is back yonder some'ers. We'll be taking him with us soon as we ketch him. You ken help us if you want."

"Got a badge?"

"Ain't got no need for no badge." He patted his rifle. "This here is all the badge I need. Now move aside, or help us. One or the other. We aim to teach him a lesson."

Mabry shook his head. "Nope. I don't think so."

The honcho looked back at the other two men. "You hear that, Silas? He don't think so." He turned back to face Mabry. "In case you can't count none, we're three to your one. You ain't thinking about besting all three of us, are you? Ole Silas over there would ventilate you in a hurry. If'n I didn't get you first. Why make a fuss over a damned Mexican?"

The Mexican then stepped out to stand beside Mabry. The rifle was pointed by the man called Silas.

"The odds are a little better now, don't you think?" Mabry asked. "I won't stand by and see anyone get lynched, whether they're Mexicans, Irishmen, or Republicans." He stood easy on his feet, his arms hanging limp at his sides. He'd learned long ago to stay calm, to relax his muscles, and to eliminate the tension in his body when trouble was at hand. And he was making no miscalculation; trouble was at hand here and now.

"Let me make this as clear as I can," Mabry said, taking two steps away from the honcho. "You're not going to take this man as long as I've got a say in it. If you want to make a fight of it, then have at it. You're going down first, then Silas next."

The honcho scratched at his unkempt bearded face. He looked over at his two riding partners, then back at Mabry. "We might have somethin' to say 'bout that," he said.

"So far, all I've seen out of you is talk."

"Come on, Riker, let's go," the third rider said. "It ain't worth a killing. Let's ride out of here."

Mabry noticed the nervousness in the man's voice. This one didn't want a fight. Mabry made a mental note this man would be the last of the three to go down if it came to a showdown.

"Shut up, Scruggs. It weren't your sister he was disabusing."

Mabry took another step back and whispered to the Mexican, "You take Silas. I'll take Riker."

"Let's not waste any more time talking," Mabry said to Riker. "You've interrupted my sleep long enough. You either make your play and we'll see how it turns out, or you ride out in one piece. Your move."

Riker rubbed his mouth with the back of his hand. Mabry knew the man was studying the odds. Riker smiled and started to turn away. He took one step, then swung his rifle around. Mabry dropped to one knee, drew his gun, and fired all in one split second. The bullet hit Riker in the shirt pocket. Mabry then swung his gun around toward Silas, but he was too late. The Mexican had already knocked Silas off his horse with a hole in his chest. The two shots had sounded as one.

The third man had thrown up his hands. "Don't shoot, don't shoot. It weren't my sister he was messing with."

Mabry went over to the two men. Both were stone dead. He holstered his gun and waited a few seconds for his nerves to calm. He pointed a finger at the third rider. "Load up these men, and get 'em out of here. Now."

The man wasted no time in draping the two dead men over their horses. He had them lashed on and was gone in less than five minutes.

Mabry turned to the stranger and asked, "They were going to hang you because you were courting one of their sisters?"

The man shrugged. "Riker caught me, how do you say? With my pants down?"

Mabry couldn't keep from grinning at the man's confession. "Are there any more brothers out there I need to know about?"

"No, *señor*. The two dead ones are Tana's brothers, Silas and Riker. I do not know the other man."

"Well, come on over to the fire if you've a mind to. I've got coffee in the pot and sleep will be a long time coming after this."

It was difficult for Mabry to get a good look at the man in the darkness. He appeared to be around thirty years old with dark skin and long black hair. He was well dressed in a Mexican-style outfit: tight black pants, and a short spangled jacket. Both of them adorned with numerous silver decorations. A *vaquero* maybe?

Mabry threw some more sticks on the fire, then fanned at the low flames with his hat. "I'll have the coffee warmed up in a few minutes."

The man handed Mabry the rifle. "Thank you, *señor*. You saved my life."

"Maybe you should be more careful with your choice of lady friends in the future."

"Sometimes it is not so easy when a beautiful *señorita* catches your eye."

Mabry reached over and poured the stranger a cup of coffee, then stuck out his hand. "My name is Frank Mabry."

The stranger took Mabry's hand and said, "My name is Rivero Vasquez. I was born in Mexico, but have lived and worked in Texas many years. I have heard of the Texas Ranger named Frank Mabry."

"Ex-Ranger now, Rivero."

The Mexican finished his coffee in silence, then said, "Thank you, *Señor* Mabry, for your hospitality. Now I must go find my horse. He is a good one. Not one to lose. I have work waiting for me down the line, so I must travel." He gave Mabry a casual salute and said, "*Adios*, my friend, and thank you."

With that, Rivero Vasquez hurried along the creek bank and disappeared into the darkness. Mabry hoped he wasn't going to return to Tana and start this hoo-rah all over again.

CHAPTER FIVE

Mabry arrived in Dallas, Texas, late Wednesday evening. The town had a hectic, hurried air about it. There were horsemen, horse-drawn carriages, and pedestrians darting here and there wherever he looked. Some were dressed in expensive-looking clothes, most were not. Red and white checked shirts, jeans, and cowhide vests seemed to rule the day. Dallas had been the location of Marshal Bannister's headquarters for two years. On paper, Bannister and his three deputy marshals worked out of the Dallas office. Mabry, like the others, was seldom seen around the office for more than a day here and there. Most often they were out on the trail chasing after evildoers.

Mabry had been puzzled why Bannister would ask to meet him at the Cattleman's Hotel and not at the office. It wasn't like Bannister to turn loose department money for a luxury like the Cattleman's Hotel. The hotel was located two blocks from the railroad depot. A young boy ran out from a lean-to and took hold of Moses' reins. After Mabry had retrieved his rifle and bags, the boy led the horse to the rear of the hotel.

The hotel lobby was filled with polished brass fixtures, cushioned furniture, and mirrors of every shape and size. Any direction he turned, Mabry got to see a reflection of how shabby looking he'd become chasing after Ryan. He stood at the registration desk more than a little self-conscious of his appearance after seeing himself in so many mirrors.

He'd never stayed at the Cattleman's Hotel on his own dime.

His meager salary didn't lend itself to the finer establishments. On his infrequent overnight stays in Dallas, he had always boarded at the Maynard Hotel, a rundown rooming house near the red light district. But that minor detail had never bothered him too much.

He tapped the service bell and gazed around the lobby while he waited for the clerk.

"May I help you?"

Mabry turned around and faced a young dark-haired woman. She smiled and said, "I assume you need a room."

"You might check your records, ma'am. Marshal Reed Bannister might've already made the arrangements. My name is Frank Mabry."

She scanned the registration book for a moment, then said, "Yes, Mr. Mabry, you're right. Please sign the book and I'll get you a key. You're assigned to room 204."

After he'd signed the register, Mabry ran a finger up the page. Bannister was in room 202. He thought it might be prudent for him to take a bath and shave off his stubble before knocking on Bannister's door. While he was rolling this around in his mind, the desk clerk handed him an envelope along with his room key.

"Mr. Bannister left this message for you."

He recognized Bannister's distinctive writing on the outside of the envelope. He tore it open and read the note:

Come to room 202 as soon as you arrive.

Bannister

So much for making himself presentable. He turned left at the top of the stairs along a wide hallway and knocked on the door of room 202. It opened on the second knock. A tall, thin man of around fifty years stood there with his hand extended. He was dressed in a rumpled black business suit complete with a white shirt, vest, and string tie. Mabry thought Reed Bannister looked mighty uncomfortable. He didn't think he'd ever seen his boss all spruced up like a big-city banker.

"You got here quick, Frank," Bannister said. "Come on in."

"What're we doing meeting in a place like this? Can you afford it? You're always crying about your penny-pinching budget."

Bannister waved a hand around the room. "It's a government paid room. So is yours. I might just stay here for a couple of days since the army's paying for it. I'll tell Rosie I'm off chasing Caddo Bill, or something."

The room was not plush, but it was filled with sufficient furniture, and was a sight better than most rooms Mabry had seen in his travels. And he ranked it higher than the hayloft and the grove of willow trees. All he'd ever required was a soft bed, a washstand with a pitcher full of water, and a clean towel. Anything else he considered a luxury.

"What's so important that you sent for me? Couldn't Gabe Rickard, or Freddie Sanchez handle it? I was supposed to help Woodrow at the ranch for a few days. And what's the deal with the army putting us up in this castle?"

"You'll find out in a few minutes. There's some men I want you to meet." Bannister took hold of Mabry's arm and said, "These men have traveled all the way from Washington to talk to us. They're in a room down the hall."

CHAPTER SIX

The two lawmen walked down the hallway to room 212 and tapped on the door. Bannister had told Mabry that Hiram Mc-Dougal, the Secretary of War's top advisor in Washington, had made the long trip to talk to them face to face. After a moment standing in the hallway, they were invited to enter the room by a man with a hoarse-sounding voice. The room they entered was well lighted and seemed to be twice as large as Bannister's room. But then, the bill for this room was being paid by the government, too.

"Senator," Bannister said, by way of greeting McDougal.

McDougal sat at a small rectangular desk with a quill ink pen in his hand. A ream of official-looking paper was scattered on the desk in front of him. He made no effort to acknowledge their presence. McDougal continued with his writing as if they were not in the room.

Mabry stood at the door and watched. McDougal didn't seem to be in any hurry, so he leaned against the door jamb and waited. He'd heard of the ex-senator and his congressional exploits. McDougal's face was fleshy, with double chins, and was crisscrossed with a map of blood vessels that suggested a lifelong attraction to the bottle. He had a mass of flowing white hair swept back over his head, resembling the sails of a seagoing schooner.

Mabry had heard rumors McDougal had been ousted from congress after taking too many unpopular stances within his own party. He supposed McDougal was another of those lifelong politicians in Washington who bounced around from one political appointment to another.

McDougal finished his writing and turned toward the visitors. "Come in, gentlemen. I apologize for making you wait. I had to finish my report before I lost my train of thought. It happens with age, you know." He stood and extended his hand as Bannister made the introduction.

"Marshal Bannister has told us many good things about you, Mabry. It appears you have lived a rather adventurous, if not downright dangerous, life. All his stories about your encounters with Indians and outlaws were most interesting."

"The marshal has a way of gilding the lily sometimes, Mr. McDougal."

They were still making small talk when two uniformed men entered through the doorway of an adjoining room. Bannister pushed Mabry toward the two men.

"Frank, meet Colonel Otis Floyd and Lieutenant Julian Keener. These officers are here as representatives of the War Department." Bannister turned back to Mabry and said, "Frank Mabry, my top deputy."

Colonel Floyd was the taller of the two officers and looked to be in his sixties. He had a grizzled appearance that reminded Mabry of a picture he'd once seen of General William Tecumseh Sherman. His hair was short, black, and stuck out in all directions. His long, slender face sported a grizzled black beard that was speckled with flecks of gray.

Lieutenant Keener was the opposite of Floyd. He was shorter, standing maybe five feet ten inches tall in his boots, and dressed in a spotless army uniform. He was well-groomed, from his sandy-colored hair down to his well-polished black boots. As Mabry got a closer look at the lieutenant, it was hard for him to believe he was an officer in the army. The young lieutenant more closely resembled a red-cheeked schoolboy, all bright-eyed and bushy-tailed. He was around twenty-four, twenty-five years old, if that.

"Sit down, gentlemen," Hiram McDougal said. "There are drinks available on the side table if you're so inclined."

There was a rattling of chairs as Mabry, Bannister, and Lieutenant Keener each took a chair around a small circular table. McDougal returned to his seat at the desk. Colonel Floyd remained standing, his hands clasped behind his back. It appeared that Colonel Floyd was the man to do the talking.

McDougal nodded toward Floyd and said, "Colonel Floyd has the information that we traveled fifteen hundred miles to present. If you please, Colonel."

CHAPTER SEVEN

Mabry got himself prepared to listen, as did the others. Colonel Floyd paced the floor while he gathered his thoughts, then moved over in front of a window and leaned back against the sill. The sun shining at his back made him an imposing figure.

"It was eight and a half months ago when the incident occurred," Floyd said. "The B and L train began its cross-country journey in Philadelphia. This westbound train had a special boxcar situated in the middle of its passenger and freight car line. The special car looked identical to any other freight car in the line by design. The train reached St. Louis on schedule where another train was waiting to haul the car on to Denver, the final leg of the journey."

Floyd smiled and turned his gaze toward Hiram McDougal. "The plan looked good on paper. Right, Hiram? Similar runs had been made dozens of times since the end of the war. Everyone thought this one would be no different. The top railway officials, General Trowbridge, and even the Secretary of War himself, had signed off on the transfer as routine business. Two tough, experienced troopers had been sent along as escorts for the journey."

Floyd hesitated for a moment, then said, "Then the whole damned shipment was stolen right from under our noses. Half a million dollars in banknotes and newly minted gold coins."

"Stolen in a brazen daytime robbery," McDougal said. The ex-senator's face was beet red as he slapped his palm on the desk. "The thought of it still makes me angry." He sat back in his chair, then looked over at Colonel Floyd. "I'm sorry for the interruption, Colonel. Please go on."

Colonel Floyd referred to a notebook he had pulled from his blouse. "The banknotes were in various denominations: tens, twenties, and fifties primarily. They are generally known around the country as greenbacks. The gold coins were largely of the twenty-dollar variety. The shipment was to be dropped at Denver to be distributed among the western governmental agencies as required for army and governmental transactions in the region."

"Five hundred thousand dollars," Mabry said, as he let out a soft whistle. "You said it was stolen right from under your noses. How? Where?"

"The train had been traveling in mountainous terrain as it neared Denver. It had slowed to a crawl on a severe uphill grade. To make things worse, the train had taken on two flatcars in St. Louis that carried heavy mining equipment. That addition to the train made the uphill climb even slower than normal. The subsequent investigation revealed that the thieves had been camped alongside the tracks for several days. We suspect they'd been watching other trains climb the uphill grade to get their timing down. When our train came along, the thieves crashed through the boxcar door with a thick oak ram. They caught the troopers off guard and took command of the car without firing a shot. The whole incident had been well-planned, well-coordinated, and well-executed. They transferred the currency to their waiting wagons while the train continued to move upgrade at a snail's pace. The engineer, conductors, firemen—even the passengers—were unaware the train had been robbed. The theft wasn't discovered until the train stopped to take on water several miles down the track."

"What happened to the two guards?"

"Killed, Mr. Mabry. Both of them in a most brutal, needless manner. It was a barbaric act. The theft was bad enough, but murder . . ." Floyd shook his head. "Their bodies were found among the trees where the thieves had made their camp. The thieves made certain they left no witnesses."

There was an awkward silence for a moment, then Floyd continued. "I have a strong suspicion it was an inside job, which makes it all the more troubling. All aspects of the journey from the initial planning, loading, travel schedule, and everything else about the shipment, was known by no more than a handful of people."

"Have you identified any suspects?"

"No, we haven't," Floyd said, with a shake of his head. "It could have been a railroad official, or heaven forbid, even one of our own officers, or administrators. We don't know at this point who it might've been. As you gentlemen well know, people will talk. There's no such thing as a secret when more than one person knows anything. It could have been anyone."

Mabry knew well the truth of that comment.

Hiram McDougal went to the side table and poured himself a tumbler of whiskey. He took a sip of the whiskey, then said, "Colonel Floyd and I have a slight disagreement on that point, gentlemen. He sees conspiracies behind every bush. He says it might have been an inside job, which it could have been, I suppose. However, I believe the robbery can be laid at the feet of those outlaws who have made life miserable for the railroads since the war ended. Scoundrels such as those killers who rode with William Quantrill, or Butcher John Burke. It's my belief it was a gang like that who got lucky and accidently hit the jackpot with this train."

"May I add a comment, sir?" Lieutenant Keener asked.

"Of course, Lieutenant."

"A team of B and L railroad detectives investigated the theft for several weeks. They questioned everyone who had direct knowledge of the transfer, and many more who were on the periphery. They wrote their reports and then moved on to other business without resolving the issue. Secretary of War Greenwell isn't satisfied with the investigation thus far, nor is the president. Secretary Greenwell wants results, and he wants them sooner rather than later."

"I don't understand why we're here in Dallas discussing this robbery," Mabry said. "I'm sure you're concerned about losing the money and the death of the soldiers, yet the robbery occurred hundreds of miles away in Colorado." He nodded at Bannister and added, "How do we fit into the picture?"

Colonel Floyd glanced at Hiram McDougal before he explained. "Hiram and I differ on this point as well. He thinks we should be concentrating our efforts in the Kansas–Missouri border area where those gangs he mentioned are known to hide. I, on the other hand, have reason to believe those responsible for the robbery left Colorado and came this direction."

"And that reason is?" Mabry asked.

"Captain Quint Rainey, an officer from Fort Leavenworth, had been assigned the task of finding these men. He had run into roadblock after roadblock all along the way. Then he must have found something that led him to Texas. A week ago Captain Rainey reported to Secretary Greenwell directly that he might've learned something important about the robbery. He told the secretary he was going to Texas and would report back later with details. That's when Secretary Greenwell sent Hiram and me out here. We were sent to find out what Rainey had discovered."

McDougal shook his head and said, "I'm afraid we arrived too late. Two days ago, Captain Rainey's body was found in a roadside ditch near Leighton, Texas. Rainey had been traveling south and had been shot two times from ambush. We have no idea where he was going, or why."

Colonel Floyd pointed toward Marshal Bannister. "Secretary Greenwell suggested that we get the local marshals involved. You men know the country better than anyone else. Marshal Bannister told us that you, Deputy Marshal Mabry, were the best man for the job. We don't have any more information that might be of help to you. However, I'm confident that Captain Rainey had learned something along the way that got him killed."

"Where is Captain Rainey's body now?" Mabry asked.

"It's in Leighton being prepared for transport back to Fort Nelson, then on to Denver from there," Floyd said. "It will be there another day until the undertaker can arrange shipment. We sent a new uniform to the undertaker."

"Can you send a message to the undertaker and ask him to keep the clothes Captain Rainey was wearing when he was killed?"

"If you think it's important to do so."

Mabry shrugged. "Who knows what's important at this stage, Colonel? Since Leighton was where Captain Rainey ended his investigation, it seems the sensible place for me to start mine."

"I'll make the arrangements," Floyd said.

Mabry began to pace around the room. He pointed at the badge on his vest and said, "I can't go chasing around the country wearing a badge and expect to find out anything. Captain Rainey must have given himself away with his uniform."

"How about going in as a cattle buyer," Bannister said. "No one would suspect you're a lawman if you act the part of a buyer. They're all around cattle country these days."

Mabry thought about it, then dismissed it as an option. He didn't think being a cattle buyer would give him the freedom to nose around and ask questions. He shook his head. "No, Reed, I don't think that would work. I think maybe I should go to

Leighton as a drifter looking for work. That'll give me more freedom to talk to strangers in a saloon, or on a street corner. I'll just be one more drifter among a large crowd of drifters."

"That makes sense to me," Colonel Floyd said.

"However Mabry wants to go about it suits me fine. His judgment on these matters tends to be sound and effective." Bannister then said, "But don't you take any unnecessary chances, you hear? Anyone, or any group, who would kill three men in cold blood makes for a dangerous bunch. Remember that."

"I'll make sure Secretary Greenwell is kept advised of your investigation," McDougal said. "You know there's a growing concern in high places about our military losing that money. There's all kinds of talk around the halls of congress about incompetency and calls for resignations here and there. It'll die down after a while as it always does. In the meantime, you need to keep a sharp eye out for any development. Make certain I stay informed. Secretary Greenwell has asked Colonel Floyd to stay in the Dallas area in case he is needed."

"One final thing, Mabry," Colonel Floyd said. "While the recovery of the currency is important to all of us, it is secondary to your assignment. If you make any kind of currency recovery, well and good. It's the men who killed the soldiers we want above all else. You bring in the men who killed the three soldiers, we will be most appreciative."

McDougal motioned toward the door. "I think that's all for tonight. Good luck to you, Mr. Mabry," he said, extending his hand. "And to you, Lieutenant Keener. I pray the two of you make convincing out-of-work drifters."

Mabry jerked his head over at Marshal Bannister. "You mean . . ."

Bannister raised a hand and whispered, "We'll talk about it later."

Lieutenant Julian Keener looked at Mabry, smiled, and said, "I'm ready to leave whenever you are, sir."

CHAPTER EIGHT

Mabry gripped his boss's arm after they had returned to Bannister's room and held on tight to prevent the marshal from walking away. Mabry had a few things on his mind, and Bannister was going to hear him out.

"Listen to me, Reed," Mabry shouted. "Lieutenant Keener isn't cut out for this kind of country, or this kind of job. He's way out of his element. He's a desk soldier at best. What were you and Colonel Floyd thinking, turning him loose out here? This could get dangerous in the blink of an eye. Think of what happened to Captain Rainey. Now you're saddling me with this rosy-cheeked kid. It's going to be hard enough to watch out for myself without watching out for him, too."

"I told them you'd feel this way and argued on your behalf. McDougal and Floyd were adamant about Lieutenant Keener going along. They won't have it any other way. With all the money that's at stake, they want one of their own along to watch over things."

"They don't trust me?"

"I don't know if they trust you or not. It doesn't change anything, either way. You'll have to accept it as a done deal and move on from there."

Mabry released Bannister's arm and sat down on the edge of the bed. He raised his hands to his face and scratched at his week's growth. "If the army is so adamant about sending someone along with me, then get me a hard-nosed major, or even better, a beefy, broad-shouldered sergeant who's been in a scrap or two. Not a wet-behind-the-ears kid, for heaven's sake."

"Lieutenant Keener is the man they chose. You can argue until you're blue in the face and it won't change a thing. Lieutenant Julian Keener is going with you. The Secretary of War said so, Colonel Floyd said so, and I say so."

Mabry soon realized the futility of his objections. The baby-faced lieutenant was going with him. He threw up his hands and said, "All right, Reed. If it's gotta be, it's gotta be. You make sure everyone understands the kid has to follow my lead. And if he gets hurt, you do the explaining."

"Quit calling him a kid. Julian Keener is an officer of the United States Army. A West Point man. Colonel Floyd tells me he's quite capable and intelligent. He assures me that he's a quick learner and tougher than he looks."

"I don't believe this is a training exercise, Reed."

"I keep telling you to think positive."

"All right. I'm positive this isn't a training exercise."

Bannister threw up his hands. "Look at me, Frank. I know you well enough to know you can handle anything you run across, so quit complaining. Look at it as one of life's little challenges."

"A challenge? Keeping us both alive is going to be more than a damned challenge."

Bannister held out an envelope. "Here's enough army money to take care of you and Lieutenant Keener in style for a few weeks. Now get outta here. I don't want to waste my army-paid amenities arguing with you."

Mabry snatched the envelope out of Bannister's hand and said, "You can bet your army-paid ass Rosie is going to hear about your amenities. See how you handle that challenge."

Chapter Nine

An hour after everyone had left Hiram McDougal's room, Colonel Otis Floyd returned. McDougal liked to tell people he was the secretary's most trusted advisor. Colonel Floyd wasn't so sure it was true; he viewed McDougal as just another political hanger-on who had been ousted from congress after being a disaster as a U.S. Senator. McDougal had shuffled around Washington in various capacities until his old friend, Secretary Greenwell, took him into the Department of War.

"Have a chair, Colonel," McDougal said. "Tell me what you think about this fiasco. Secretary Greenwell wants a full report, as does the president."

"Mabry seems to be the man for the job, although I can't say with full confidence that he has any expectation of finding either the money or the murderers."

"Yes, I would agree. I understand Mabry has quite the reputation for getting things done, so maybe he will surprise us. He was one of those tough Texas Rangers at one time, I believe."

"That's my understanding as well. Marshal Bannister ranks him high."

McDougal let out a sigh. "He has a tough task ahead of him."

Floyd walked around the desk and stood near the window. "We'll have to take Bannister's word about Mabry's abilities. We decided—that is, Secretary Greenwell and you, decided—that we wouldn't leave anything to chance. We requested the best man Bannister could provide. Bannister's and Mabry's reputations should cover the department's backside if we're not successful in bringing the killers to justice. You were clear you didn't want any room for second-guessing from congressmen, or newspapermen."

"Yes, getting the best people was imperative. We want this problem resolved, one way or the other. It has become a distraction to the secretary."

"I feel some sense of security by sending a pair of our own eyes along to keep us informed. Lieutenant Keener is an ambitious young officer who will serve our purposes well."

"I know Lieutenant Keener's father, Judge Endicott Keener, rather well," McDougal said. "He's a hard-nosed man who won't stand for any missteps in his courtroom."

"I'm told Lieutenant Keener is cut from the same cloth, just younger and less experienced. I chose him because of those traits, even though there were more qualified men available."

"I hope you made the correct decision, Colonel. I would hate for anything to happen to Judge Keener's son."

"So would I. To repeat, all of us want this affair to be beyond criticism. Who better to be in front than the son of an esteemed judge if it fails?"

McDougal smiled. "You've thought of everything, haven't you?"

"Maybe, maybe not. The unfortunate death of Captain Rainey might mean we're making progress. After eight months, his cryptic message was the first indication we've had that has given us any hope."

McDougal stood and walked to the door. "What are the chances that Mabry can find the killers?"

Colonel Floyd, knowing the meeting was over, followed him. "I'd say less than fifty-fifty. According to Bannister, too much time has passed. The thieves have had eight months to cover their trail."

McDougal pushed Floyd through the door and said, "Good night, Colonel. Keep me informed." McDougal turned toward the side table. "Now I must prepare myself for that damnable trip back to Washington City. One bottle of Scotch should do it."

CHAPTER TEN

The next morning, Mabry found Lieutenant Keener waiting for him in the hotel lobby. The young officer was dressed as impeccably as one could be in his dark-blue wool uniform. He stood as Mabry approached him from the stairway.

"I heard your shouting match with Marshal Bannister last evening," Keener said. "As did half the people in the hotel. You made it quite clear how you feel about me going along with you. You were pretty vocal in your opinion that I would be more of a hindrance to you than a help."

"Since you heard it, I can't try to deny it, can I? It appears you got the gist of the discussion correct. This is no job for an untried newcomer to the territory. I'll say this as a reminder to both of us. Three men we know about have already died because of this train robbery. I don't doubt for a second there will be others dead before we finish. I'll tell you the same thing I told the marshal: I'll have enough trouble keeping myself alive without having to watch after you."

Keener glared at Mabry and said, "Colonel Floyd made it clear that I was to go along on this mission, and to assist you in every aspect of it. So let's get things straight right now before we start. Those were my orders, and I intend to obey those orders to the fullest extent possible. If you feel the need to be in charge and call the shots, that's fine with me. That was another of Colonel Floyd's orders. However, if I think you're wrong, I'll say so in no uncertain terms. I understand the dangers that could be in front of us and I'm prepared to face them head-on."

"That's good to know, Lieutenant. I pray that you can hold up your end."

"And along the way, Mr. Mabry, I will endeavor to impart to you a much needed lesson in manners and respect that you seem to be lacking."

Mabry noticed the young officer's face had a tendency to get red as he became angry. And it was plenty red now. He didn't mind the anger, but he would keep a close eye on the young lieutenant to see how he reacted when the chips were down.

"And so you'll know what lies ahead, Lieutenant, let me tell you about the men I generally pursue. They're bad men who cheat and don't play by the rules. They don't stand in formation and they don't wear bright red hats. They're partial to sneaking up on a man in the dark with a sharp Bowie knife, or taking potshots at him from behind a tree or rock when he's not looking."

"Go ahead, make your little jokes, Mabry. Just remember one thing; you have me with you, so you might as well make the best of it."

"I assure you I'm not making little jokes, Lieutenant. I'm as serious as a rattlesnake in your blanket."

As much as it bothered him, Mabry had to face the reality of the situation. Lieutenant Keener was correct in what he had said; Keener was going with him whether he wanted him along or not. Mabry hoped and prayed he could keep both of them alive for the duration of their partnership.

"It's good that we both know how we stand," Mabry said. "Right now, we don't need to waste any more time talking. We need to go clothes shopping. You've got to get rid of that spiffy army uniform you're wearing. That blue uniform will draw all kinds of unwanted attention where we're going. In fact, it might've gotten your Captain Rainey killed."

Mabry took Lieutenant Keener to the nearby shops where they bought boots, denim pants, shirts, bandannas, and every other item they could find to make Keener's transformation from a rigid army officer to a loose-legged drifting cowboy. Then they crossed the street to a gun shop. The shop smelled of gunpowder, gun grease, and cured leather. The shopkeeper was a lean, wiry man who wore a black patch over his left eye. He was tinkering with a rifle when they entered.

"Welcome, gents," the shopkeeper said, not looking up from his work. "You see anything you want, let me know."

There were hundreds of choices: Henrys, Winchesters, and Spencers. Navy Colts, Remingtons, and a few brands Mabry had never seen before. "We're kinda short on cash right now," Mabry said. "Do you have a Colt handgun that's in right good condition you might sell for a reasonable price?"

The shopkeeper laid the rifle aside, put his hand to his chin, and thought it over. "Give me a minute," he said, as he disappeared behind a curtain at the rear of his shop.

Mabry strolled around the shop, taking a look at the new merchandise. He hadn't been in a gun store in some time. The old Colt he wore was like a friend who had stood by him for years during the good times and the bad. He wasn't about to let that friend down by replacing him with a newer model. A new Winchester standing in a rack caught his eye. He put it to his shoulder, swung it around left to right, and aimed it at a deer head hanging on the far wall.

"Nice feel," he said to Keener. Mabry replaced the rifle in the rack and continued to stroll around the shop. After a few minutes, the shopkeeper returned and laid a well-worn, single-action Colt .45 on the desk. Mabry picked it up while Keener peered over his shoulder. He rolled the cylinder, hefted the gun in his hands a couple of times, and looked down the barrel.

"Grips are kinda wore down," Mabry said. "And she looks a little banged up."

"It's a good gun," the shopkeeper said. "I bought it direct from the grieving widow." He reached into a drawer, took out a handful of cartridges, and motioned to the rear of the store. "Here, take a few of these cartridges out back and give her a try."

Mabry had seen all he needed to see. He knew it was a good serviceable gun; the kind of gun a wandering cowboy looking for work would carry. "How much you asking?"

"Seeing's how I ain't had time to clean it up none, I guess I could let you have it for, say, twenty-five dollars."

Mabry reached into his pocket and pulled out a wad of money and a few coins. He counted it out on the bench in front of the shopkeeper. When he had finished counting, he pushed the whole pile toward the shopkeeper and said, "I'll give you eighteen dollars and . . . let's see . . . twenty-seven cents—if you'll throw in that old gun belt and holster over there."

The man stuck out his hand. "Done," he said. "I'll even throw in half a box of cartridges."

They went back to the hotel room, where Mabry watched Keener put on his new outfit. Keener appeared to be a fine specimen of a man when he took off the uniform. He had wide shoulders, a trim narrow waist, and well-defined muscles. Still, he didn't look right when he had dressed in his new outfit. Now he looked to be what he really was: an Easterner in brand-new western clothes. And that wasn't how he needed to look for their purposes.

"Come on, kid. We're going shopping again."

"What do you mean?" Keener asked, as he waved his hand around at the sacks and boxes scattered around the hotel room.

"What else could I need?"

"Follow me and I'll show you."

CHAPTER ELEVEN

Deputy Marshal Mabry and Lieutenant Keener left the hotel and headed toward the stockyard where the holding pens were bustling with bawling cattle. Cowboys milled around: some sitting on the railings, others grouped together talking and smoking cigarettes. The smell of coal smoke drifted over from the railyard. Specks of black cinder and gray ash dotted their shirts.

Mabry held up a hand and stopped. He looked around, then spotted a cowboy who looked to be a perfect fit for their needs. The cowboy was standing near a corral scraping the mud off his boots with a stick. He wore denim pants that were frayed at the cuffs, a dingy blue-striped shirt faded with age, and down at the heel black boots.

Perfect.

"Go over and stand beside that cowboy, kid."

Keener turned to the deputy marshal, his cheeks bright red again. "Let's get something straight right now, Mr. Mabry. My name is not *kid*. I would appreciate it if you would stop calling me that. I know you're the tough westerner with a big reputation, but would you please show me a modicum of respect? You may call me, Keener, Julian, lieutenant, or even Jefferson, my middle name." Then he raised his voice a notch and shouted, "But stop with the damned kid stuff."

Mabry pursed his lips at Keener's obvious sincerity and passion. "I can't call you lieutenant, that's for sure. Your choice."

"Then how about calling me Jeff. That's what my friends call me. Although it would be a stretch to call you a friend at this point."

"Jeff it is—unless I forget every now and then. You can forget the mister stuff, too. Most people just call me plain ol' Mabry."

Jeff stared at him for a moment in silence, then marched over toward the cowboy as Mabry had requested.

"Hey, what's going on here?" the cowboy asked as Keener sidled up beside him. "You two looking for trouble?"

"No, no," Mabry said. "We're not looking for trouble at all. Truth be known, it's your lucky day." He pointed at Jeff, who appeared to be the exact size of the cowboy. "See those duds he's wearing? He feels extra bad about wearing new store-bought clothes when a hardworking cowboy such as yourself has to make do with . . . with . . . well, you know what I'm talking about."

"Nope. I don't understand a whit what you're talking about," the cowboy said. "You ain't making a lick of sense."

"Let me explain," Mabry said, as he laid a hand on Jeff's shirt. "Jeff here is offering to trade his new store-bought clothes for your clothes. Even up. No tricks. What do you say about that?"

The cowboy looked Keener up and down, then asked, "You mean you want to swap those clothes you're wearing, for these here clothes I'm wearing?"

Keener rolled his eyes and said, "That's what the man said."

"Boots, too?"

"Yep, the boots, too," Mabry said. "He'll even trade that handsome gray Stetson he's wearing for your old beat-up water bucket."

The cowboy took Jeff by the arm and pushed him toward a barn. "Damnedest trade I ever did hear of," he said, grinning from ear to ear.

It took them ten minutes to make the swap. The change in

Lieutenant Keener's appearance was remarkable. Keener reappeared looking like a real-live cowpuncher.

"There's no cowboy law somewhere that says I can't wash these stinking clothes, is there?" Jeff asked.

"Nope, not that I ever heard of." As Jeff got closer, Mabry backed away from him, turned his head, and added, "In fact, I'd recommend it."

CHAPTER TWELVE

Elbert's Mortuary and Barber Shop in Leighton, Texas, was housed in a one-story clapboard building. Its whitewashed siding had brown vertical streaks where the wood had soaked up the whitewash. The building had a wide porch in front complete with two wooden benches.

Mabry and Keener dismounted in front of the mortuary two days after leaving Dallas. They each carried the appearance of a down-on-his-luck cowpuncher out looking for his next meal. Mabry scratched at his stubble and glanced around the small town as he fiddled with his saddle. He doubted they were being watched, but he'd learned long ago it paid to be watchful.

"You can stay here or join me inside," Mabry said. "Whichever."

"I'll stay out here and watch for anyone who seems to have an interest in us."

A bell tingled above Mabry's head as the door to the mortuary opened. The waiting room was dark and dreary, befitting its calling. Several straight-backed chairs were scattered around, as were vases of paper flowers faded with age. He spotted a barber's chair over in the corner near a wide window, the other half of Elbert's enterprise. Mabry guessed the death trade in Leighton wasn't sufficient for the undertaker's needs.

A tall, heavyset man dressed in dark pants and white shirt appeared from behind a curtained doorway. He took a look at Mabry and said, "I expect you want a shave and haircut. Am I right, stranger? I'm Elias Elbert, barber, mortician, part-time animal doctor, and mayor of this fine town."

Mabry ran a hand over his emerging beard and thought, yep, I guess I do need a shave and haircut. Instead he replied, "Not today. I came to pick up the clothes that Captain Rainey was wearing when he was killed. I understand you have them."

"Ahh, yes. A terrible thing. A fine-looking young officer like Captain Rainey shot down while minding his own business. They never found the man who shot him. Are you a relative?"

Mabry shook his head. "Just a friend."

"Sheriff Laney thought it might have been a robbery attempt, since your friend looked like a prosperous man."

"What do you mean, robbery attempt?" Mabry asked. "Do you mean there was no actual robbery?"

"Well . . . What I meant . . . well . . ."

"Was there an actual robbery, or wasn't there?" Mabry asked, with a little more force to his voice.

Elbert hesitated, then said, "All I know is what I heard. That's all."

"I want to see Captain Rainey's personal belongings. Now."

"Well, I . . . I . . ."

Mabry stepped in closer and took hold of Elbert by the front of his shirt. "How about it, undertaker? If there was no robbery, there had to be money and other personal items on Captain Rainey when he died. I want them along with his clothes."

Elbert stammered and stuttered, then said, "They're in back. I was going to send them to Fort Nelson later."

"Sure you were."

The undertaker opened a desk drawer in the back room and pulled out a small brown-paper bag. He handed it to Mabry. "Here's what was on the deceased when he arrived at my mortuary. If there's anything missing, you'll have to see Sheriff Laney about it."

Mabry opened the bag and looked inside. He found a few coins and a leather wallet holding the captain's identification papers. There was a single twenty-dollar banknote in the wallet. Nothing else.

"All right, Elbert," Mabry said. "Where's the rest of the money?"

The undertaker's face was popping out with sweat, and his voice was beginning to tremble. "I was going to send it back. Honest."

Mabry waited.

The undertaker backed away, reached behind the desk, and retrieved a metal box. He searched through the box and handed an envelope to Mabry. "It's all there," he said. "Every last cent—a little more than two hundred dollars. An officer from Fort Nelson brought me a new uniform and a voucher for expenses. I'll swear that's all the money he had on him."

Mabry had no reason not to believe the undertaker this time.

"Now the clothes," Mabry said.

CHAPTER THIRTEEN

"I had my helper take the clothes to the casket shop," Elbert told Mabry. "We usually go through old clothes and use whatever we can as rags around the place. Captain Rainey's clothes were pretty bloody, so I don't know how much use they'll be to anybody. Even Sheriff Laney didn't bother to search through them they were so bloody."

"I want to see them."

Mabry followed Elbert out the back door to a small stone building. It appeared to be a workshop where wooden caskets were constructed. A man wearing a red bandanna tied around his face was busy sawing a piece of pine lumber when they entered. He was sweating profusely and covered in sawdust.

"Where's that box of clothes that belonged to the army officer?" Elbert asked.

Mabry took a look around the shop, unsure if the helper could lay his hands on the box amongst all the sawdust and scraps of lumber scattered around. The helper shook his apron free of sawdust, wiped his face with a handkerchief, and walked to the corner of the shop.

"It's over here somewhere. Gimme a minute." The carpenter tossed aside a few pieces of scrap lumber, then kicked at a black cat hiding behind a stack of planks. "Get outta here, you beggar. Ahh, here it is."

The helper handed the box to Elbert, who then passed it over to Mabry.

Mabry took the box and circled around the mortuary to the front of the building. Jeff was sitting on a bench watching the townsfolk go about their business. Mabry took a seat beside him.

"Here's the uniform Captain Rainey was wearing when he was killed. Let's go through it and see if there's anything in his pockets the sheriff might've overlooked. The undertaker had a sack full of Rainey's personal items, so it could be he wasn't searched by the killer after he was shot."

Mabry opened the box and dumped the clothes on the walkway. "Well, this is a surprise," he said. Mabry kicked at the clothes with the toe of his boot. Captain Rainey hadn't been wearing his uniform after all. He was dressed in ordinary civilian clothes. A little fancier than most, but not a uniform.

"Captain Rainey wasn't quite as dumb as you thought, was he?" Jeff said.

Mabry frowned at Keener, then began sorting the clothes on the boardwalk. The undertaker was right in his assessment. The clothes were ragged, stiff, and bloody. Mabry started his search with the trousers, while Jeff began with the captain's coat. Neither of them found anything of importance.

Mabry then bent over the white dress shirt. He lifted it up and stretched it out at arm's length. It had two pockets. The left pocket was ragged and bloody from the gunshot that had killed Rainey. He fingered both pockets, then let out a whoop.

Jeff looked up at the sound. "Did you find something?"

"Could be."

Mabry stretched the shirt out on the bench and slowly pulled at the left shirt pocket. "I think there's a piece of paper in this pocket." Mabry guessed the thin piece of paper had been overlooked because of its unpleasant, bloody location. "I hope I can get it out without destroying it."

Mabry took a deep breath, then bent over the shirt. He

inserted two fingers into the pocket, squeezed them around the paper, and slowly lifted it free of the pocket.

"Good going," Jeff said.

The small piece of paper was stiff and brittle from Rainey's dried blood. When Mabry unfolded the paper, he could see that much of the writing was blurred and faded. Still, he thought he could make out what was written on the paper. He decided to withhold his opinion until Jeff could take a look at it.

"See what you think is written on this."

Jeff took the paper and gazed at it for several seconds, then replied, "Carrsville Landing."

Mabry nodded in agreement. "Carrsville Landing," he said. "That's what I see, too."

"Do you have any idea what it means? Is there a Carrsville Landing near here?"

"I have no idea what it means. There's a town named Carrsville forty or so miles south of here. I can tell you it's not located anywhere near a river. I rode through there a time or two back when I was a Ranger. There was no river near there then, and I doubt there's one there now."

Mabry glanced at the piece of paper again. *Carrsville. Landing.* He shook his head.

Chapter Fourteen

The horseman waited in the shadows of a cottonwood grove a few miles from Carrsville. His head was never still as he looked this way and that. He had received an anonymous message to meet someone in the grove who had important information regarding Colorado. If he didn't show, the message said, the *Carrsville Recorder* would have an interesting front-page story in its next edition.

The message shook him to his very core. Who was it? Why the meeting? There were only a few people who could possibly know of his connection to the Colorado train robbery. He didn't want to meet the person who was behind the threats, yet he knew he didn't have a choice.

As vigilant as he had been, he was alarmed when he heard the sound of a voice behind him.

"Howdy, Junior."

He jerked his heard around at the sound. "Dickson!"

Coy Dickson laughed. "You were a hard man to track down, Junior. It would make a body think you didn't want to be found. But you know me. When I set out to do something, I'm pretty stubborn about it. I'd have to say you picked a place where the law is unlikely to be looking. Who in his right mind would live on a ranch out here in this godforsaken country?"

"I should have guessed it would be you. What do you want? We finished our business months ago." The horseman could feel the tremor in his hands as he glared at the outlaw who sat on a tall, sleek black stallion a few yards away. Coy Dickson was a lean, wiry man of forty years, but he had the look of a man much older. His face was narrow and craggy, filled with furrowed lines. A thin scar ran from just below his left eye to his chin: a souvenir from a Rebel saber. He stood no more than five feet seven inches tall and weighed no more than a hundred and forty pounds.

He still smarted over Dickson's disrespect during the war. It had been his unfortunate pleasure to have Sergeant Coy Dickson riding with the cavalry unit that supported the 6th Illinois Regiment. It was the 6th Illinois where he had served as an aide to General Mueller. The cavalry was commanded by the glory hound, Major Daniel Trager. General Mueller had given Trager a free hand, which had led to numerous bloody raids on the civilian population. Newspapers began to refer to Trager as the "Yankees' Bloody Bill."

The worst of Trager's men was Sergeant Coy Dickson. It had fallen on the horseman, as the general's aide, to carry out discipline on Dickson on three different occasions. He had reprimanded the sergeant once, and had reduced his rank to corporal twice. Somehow Major Trager had always thwarted his efforts and managed to get the charges against Dickson either reduced or dismissed outright. Dickson had that knowing smirk on his face each time he had stood before him, knowing whatever discipline he dished out, Major Trager would get it reversed.

Dickson infuriated him further by calling him Junior in front of the troops. Not Sir, not Colonel, but Junior. And it had stuck among the troops after they saw his reaction to the insult. Junior had heard of Dickson's exploits following the war. Dickson had taken his cavalry skills to the outlaw trail, where he rode with the Krueger Gang, Cal Hardy, and others until he decided he could do better on his own. He soon developed a reputation as a cold-blooded killer who'd never been caught.

It had galled Junior to no end that he had to track Dickson down to ask for his help. Under the circumstances, he had known of no other way—or any other person—capable of helping him pull off a train robbery in the Colorado mountains. He thought he'd seen the last of Dickson when they had parted ways after he had paid the outlaw their agreed-upon fifty thousand dollars. He should've known better.

"Me and the boys got to thinking," Dickson said. "We don't believe we got a fair cut of that government money back in Colorado. We're thinking it was us who took all the chances, and it was you who took all the money. Besides that, you held out on us. I learned from the newspapers we took half a million dollars off that train. You led us to believe it was less than half that." Dickson held out his hands. "I trusted you, Junior. I trusted you, and you let me down."

"You got every penny we had agreed on. Fifty thousand dollars. A deal is a deal."

"You forget I had to split it with four others. That money didn't last as long as I thought it would."

Junior gave out a harsh laugh. "I don't imagine it took long for you to gamble it away. You never could pass up a saloon, or a poker game."

Dickson dismounted and rolled himself a cigarette. He squatted against a tree trunk as he stared at his old nemesis. He pointed the cigarette at Junior and said, "You could have heard from us earlier, friend. But when me and the boys got here, we bumped into an old acquaintance who had a good deal going for hisself. He didn't want to let us in on it until we persuaded him it would be a good idea. In fact, we took it over and sent him on his way. He showed us another way to fill our pockets that was too good to pass up. These ranches around here are easy pickings."

"It's you and your gang who's been doing all the rustling around here?"

"Like I said, it's been easy pickings. We even took a few of yours at the beginning until we decided to leave you alone. After all, we're friends. We've about wore out our welcome now, so the boys are getting a little nervous. There's talk about the ranchers bringing in a range detective, or maybe forming a vigilante squad. We think it might be best if we moved on. We're looking for a little traveling money now. And you've got what we want."

Dickson stood, threw the butt on the ground, and walked over to Junior's horse. He took hold of the reins and gave Junior a cold, hard look. "We'll take one hundred thousand dollars and be gone in a week. We know you've got it hid away somewhere close by or you wouldn't be out here. You and your friends agreed not to spend your share for a year, right? Me and the boys ain't that particular."

Junior lowered his head as Dickson lectured him. He didn't like to be lectured—especially by a man like Coy Dickson.

Dickson pointed a finger at Junior. "You turn loose one hundred thousand dollars, and I'll guarantee you we'll be gone in a week. How's that? Then you can forget you ever knew me."

Junior knew he had few choices other than to agree to Dickson's demands. Knowing the man's violent disposition, he could very well be dead in less than a minute if he argued. Maybe later he would find a way around it, or maybe talk him down to fifty thousand.

Junior nodded at Dickson and said, "I'll see to it. It'll take me a few days to get to the money. I don't have it close at hand. One hundred thousand, and I'll never hear from you again."

Dickson swung up in the saddle, wheeled his stallion around, and galloped away. "I'll give you one week," he shouted over his shoulder. "Don't disappoint me."

CHAPTER FIFTEEN

Carrsville was a typical cow town. It had the same look about it that Mabry had seen in a hundred other small Texas towns. Carrsville had the same kinds of businesses, the same kinds of people, and most likely, the same kinds of problems.

They'd been on the trail for three days from Leighton, not hurrying, just taking in the country and getting a feel for the terrain—and to let the boyish-looking Keener take on a less clean-cut military look. His hair had begun to curl around his ears, and his face had taken on a deeper brown color.

They had stopped along the way on three occasions to let Jeff become acquainted with the grieving widow's revolver. Mabry had been surprised at the lieutenant's deft handling of the gun after the few pointers he'd given him. But it soon became clear that Jeff was more comfortable with the Winchester he had brought along with him than the revolver.

After the third shooting session with the revolver, Jeff had hit the targets Mabry had set up three out of six times. The other three had been narrow misses. Jeff glanced over at Mabry with a self-satisfied smile on his face.

"Not bad shooting," Mabry said. "You hit three tin cans—but not a one of them shot back at you."

"Do you try to be a horse's ass, Mabry? Or does it come natural to you?"

"Don't you go and get all ill-mannered on me." Mabry started to add *kid,* then thought better of it. There was no sense riling the young officer any more than necessary.

Mabry knew, for all intents and purposes, the two of them looked no different from a hundred other drifting cowboys out scouting for work. From here it was anyone's guess what might be next for them. They had to trust that somehow they might catch a break.

"We need to watch out that we don't do anything stupid and give ourselves away," Mabry said. "Keep those two army guards and Captain Rainey uppermost in your mind." Ahead, on the right side of the street, Mabry spotted the Carrsville Hotel. After being in the saddle for three days, he needed a place to light for a good night's sleep. His back was aching, as usual after a long ride, and his bottom was saddle sore. He motioned Jeff over toward the hotel.

"Let's splurge tonight and live the lives of gentlemen, what do you say? Maybe nobody will notice us staying in a hotel our first night in town."

Jeff didn't argue the point.

They dismounted in front of the hotel. Mabry took his bags and rifle from the saddle. A night of unbroken rest and sleep was what he needed. He was quite certain Jeff felt the same way. As he climbed the steps to the hotel, Mabry spotted a young woman sitting in a rocking chair on the veranda. She had thick, curly auburn hair, silky and shiny, that hung down past her shoulders. He hadn't meant to stare, yet there was something familiar about her. What was it? He touched the tip of his dusty, trail-worn hat and dipped his head in her direction.

He quickly saw the young lady's eyes were not focused on him. Her eyes were fixed on Jeff, who was close behind.

"Evening, ma'am," Jeff said.

Mabry saw a slight smile crease the young lady's lips, then she turned her head away without responding to Jeff's greeting.

Inside the lobby, Mabry walked up to a long registration desk and dropped his gear on the floor near the desk.

A small man wearing thick eyeglasses asked, "Looking for a bed, mister?"

"Yep. My partner and I need two rooms if you have them. And the use of your bathhouse, too."

"I guess we can accommodate you," the man said. "For how long?"

"One night is about all we can afford I'm afraid. Do you know of any ranches around here looking for hands?"

"That'll be four dollars for two rooms, and four bits for the baths—in advance. As for jobs, they're about as rare around here as I've ever seen. You might try the Slant-H, or the Bar-N. I hear the Bar-N has lost a few men over the past four or five months. That might be your best bet, if they're hiring. They can't pay the men they've already got from what I've been hearing."

Mabry signed the book, Frank.

CHAPTER SIXTEEN

After spending a few minutes getting their gear stowed away in their rooms, and another thirty minutes in the bathhouse, Mabry and Jeff entered the hotel's dining room. The room was large and bright with lanterns hanging all around. Mabry figured the hotel must have a good cook since the room was crowded. The conversation was loud and jovial as the patrons enjoyed their evening meal while they visited with their neighbors between bites.

Mabry spotted an empty table covered with a white tablecloth near the kitchen door. White cloth napkins had been placed in front of each chair, and a tall lighted candle sat in the center of the round table. He placed his black hat on the knob of a vacant chair next to him. Jeff laid his battered old hat on the floor beside his chair. Several of the patrons glanced in their direction. Just two more out-of-work cowboys cluttering up their town.

A frail girl with big brown eyes and a pale complexion came over to take their orders. Both of them ordered steaks: Mabry's well done, Jeff's rare. As the girl headed back to the kitchen, Mabry noticed three scruffy-looking men burst into the room. They swayed from side to side, and leaned on each other to keep from falling. Their booming voices caused everyone in the room to turn in their direction. The man in front was short, stocky, and wide through the chest. Mabry couldn't keep from staring at the beefy man. He had an oversized head that sat flat on his shoulders without benefit of a neck. He had a long, wide jaw that had seen its share of punches over the years. His prominent nose was bent sideways.

This man had the look of a brawler about him. Mabry, ever vigilant, noticed he carried a holstered gun belted around his waist, too. The two men alongside him were taller, and dressed in dirty denims and dingy, sweat-stained shirts. They carried guns as well. All three of them appeared to have had a long visit with John Barleycorn before coming to the café. Mabry kept a close eye on them as they looked around the crowded room.

The rest of the dining room patrons had stopped talking. Mabry noticed they seemed to concentrate on their plates all of a sudden. A change had come over the room.

The men eventually found a small table that was unoccupied, but had only two chairs. Two of the men stumbled over to the table and sat down, leaving the third one, the one Mabry had begun to think of as No Neck, without a chair. No Neck spotted the empty chair beside Mabry and staggered over toward him. No Neck picked up the chair without speaking, and in the process, knocked Mabry's hat to the floor.

Mabry made every effort to remain as passive as he could manage. Inside he was ready for what might come next. He'd seen it happen with drunks too often. No Neck ignored the hat, which lay on the dusty wooden floor. Mabry glanced around at the patrons and considered the situation. There were men and women of all ages in the dining room. And even a couple of youngsters. He knew they all were watching him to see what his intentions were. He mulled it over briefly, then decided to let the incident pass. He reached down, picked up the hat, and laid it on the table without comment.

The people in the dining room resumed eating with an almost audible sigh of relief. Then, as No Neck carried the pilfered chair over to join his partners, he stumbled and fell on an elderly man who was holding a cup of coffee. The coffee cup tumbled out of the man's hand and spilled its contents on his shirt. No Neck was stretched out on the table with his feet tangled up in the chair. The room went quiet again. Mabry sensed everyone was waiting to see what would happen next.

They didn't have to wait long. No Neck shoved the man backwards onto the floor and stood over him. "You clumsy old fool," he shouted, his words blurred with whiskey. "You tripped me on purpose."

The elderly man didn't back down. He pointed a finger and said, "Look here, Bascom. It was you that fell on me. I didn't trip you, and you know it."

The man called Bascom reached down and pulled the elderly man to his feet, then shoved him toward the doorway, where he fell to the floor. "Get outta here, old man."

Mabry had seen enough. He was willing to let the hat incident ride. Now this thug had gone too far with his treatment of the elderly man. He pushed away from the table and eased over to the fallen man, all the while keeping his eyes on No Neck. "Here you go, mister," he said, holding out his left hand. "Let me help you up. Now you go on back to your table and finish your supper."

The patrons began to move away from their tables. Mabry understood their thinking; their actions brought to mind a wild animal that knows by instinct there's a storm brewing on the horizon and seeks shelter. The people in the dining room seemed to know trouble was on its way.

Bascom straightened up and stared at Mabry with a wicked grin on his dark, battered face. Without a word he reached for his gun.

Mabry had anticipated No Neck's reaction and had his gun out of his holster in a flash. He slammed his revolver down on Bascom's wrist. Bascom let out a loud yelp as his gun went skidding across the floor.

Bascom took hold of his wrist with his left hand and said, "Mister, you made a terrible mistake interfering in my business."

"You're drunk and have no business in here," Mabry said. "These people are enjoying their evening meal. You're not going to ruin it for them. Now if you want to go outside and finish this dispute, I'll be more than obliged. In here we're going to let these people finish their meals in peace. Understand?"

The lawman glanced around to see if Jeff had the brawler's two friends covered. He was disappointed to see that the young officer was still seated at the table, with wide eyes staring at the melee. Mabry jerked his gun toward the two men, who were now standing with their hands poised above their holstered guns.

"Guns on the floor, you two. Now." The men looked at each other, then did as they were told.

"You can pick up your guns at the desk tomorrow. Now get outta here, all three of you."

Bascom kicked the chair out of his way and staggered toward the door. His two partners were close behind him. At the door Bascom stopped and turned toward Mabry. "We'll meet again," he said.

Mabry had no doubt they would.

CHAPTER SEVENTEEN

Mabry had almost finished his meal when he sensed someone standing behind him. He looked across the table at Jeff and could see the lieutenant staring at the unknown person. Without turning, Mabry said, "I don't like anyone standing behind me. Come on around where I can see you, whoever you are."

The man circled the table and stood in front of Mabry.

"Well, stranger," the man said. "Not everyone can face down Rad Bascom and get away with it."

"He was drunk and making a nuisance of himself," Mabry said. "Besides that, according to Bascom, I haven't gotten away with it yet. He said we'd meet again, which I don't doubt a bit. In a town this small, I don't see how we can avoid each other for very long."

"I take it you're planning to be around for a while?"

"My partner and I are job hunting. If we don't have any luck here, we'll be moving on in a few days. We'll find something somewhere if we keep looking."

Mabry lowered his coffee cup and looked up at the speaker. He judged him to be about his own size: five feet eleven, one hundred and seventy pounds, with a narrow waist and wide shoulders. He was dressed in dirty black denim pants and a red shirt that had turned pink with too many washings. The man's hair was a longish light brown, and he sported a thick, bushy brown beard that obscured most of his face. Mabry guessed him to be in his late thirties or early forties.

The dining room had cleared out by then, so Mabry got their visitor a chair, which he placed beside his. He nodded to the chair and said, "Join us for a cup of coffee, Mister—?"

"Garber," he said. "Hank Garber. I'm foreman over at the Slant-H ranch a few miles from here. Ever heard of it?"

Mabry looked over at Keener. "Not me. How about you, Jeff?"

"No. I can't say I've heard of it either."

"Then you must be new to this part of Texas if you've never heard of the Slant-H. It's one of the biggest spreads around. It's owned by Dave Harker."

"Does this Rad Bascom work for you?"

Garber cocked his head sideways. "Why would you ask that?"

"Simple enough. It's becoming pretty plain to me you're going to offer us a job riding for your outfit. I want to know what kind of people I'd be associating with if I say yes. My partner here can make up his own mind. As for me, I'm a little bit particular about who I punch cattle with."

"You're an arrogant bastard, aren't you?" Garber said, with a loud laugh. "It's no wonder you're job hunting. But you're right. That's why I came in here to talk to you. I was over at the feed store when I heard the story of your tangle with Bascom. By all the accounts I heard, you handled yourself like you knew what you were doing. I can use a man with your talents on the Slant-H. And I'll take your partner here on trial. If he proves out, I'll sign him up, too. You two be out at the Slant-H tomorrow morning ready to go to work."

Garber took a final sip of his coffee and said, "You might as well know this first. We run a tight outfit out at the Slant-H. We have rules and we don't tolerate anybody breaking 'em. Wages are paid at the end of each month: forty a month and found. You don't finish the month, you don't get anything."

Garber pushed away from the table and left the dining room in a hurry.

Jeff tossed his napkin on his plate and said, "Well now, Mabry. Don't tell me that fits into your grandiose plan of two lazy drifters out looking for work." Jeff stared at the marshal and added, "Care to tell me how we're going to roam around the countryside asking questions, if we have to go to work tomorrow morning? I'd like to hear your answer."

Mabry stared into his coffee cup. He didn't have an answer.

"We can always look at it this way," Jeff said. "Since I wouldn't know a bull from a buffalo when it comes to cattle ranching, Garber won't sign me on after the first day."

"Yep, that would probably work for me, too. The only thing is, our out-of-work drifter story goes out the window either way."

Mabry continued to stare into his coffee cup as he debated whether or not to bring up another subject that had been bothering him ever since his argument with Bascom. After thinking it over, he decided it would be best to get it out in the open.

"While we're talking, Lieutenant Keener. What did you think about that disagreement I had with Bascom a little while ago?"

"I thought you handled it rather well. He was a mean drunk and was abusing an older gentleman. I thought you showed admirable courage."

"Did you notice his two friends?"

"Of course I did. How could I miss them? They all came in together."

"And that didn't cause you to think about anything?" Mabry asked.

Jeff's cheeks began to redden as he said, "If you're trying to say something, then come right out and say it. Stop beating around the bush. I'm not good at solving riddles."

Mabry shook his head. "Never mind." He dropped money on the table and headed for the doorway into the hotel lobby. "As for this job thing, maybe you should pray for a miracle to happen tonight."

"That's a real comforting thought," Jeff said. "Expect a miracle to come along to solve our problems for us."

Chapter Eighteen

The room at the Carrsville Hotel was no match for the Cattleman's Hotel in Dallas. The washstand was wobbly, the water bowl was cracked, and the bed creaked when he sat on it. Still, it suited Mabry just fine. He felt much better after his bath and the meal, and looked forward to a peaceful night's sleep. It might well be his last opportunity for a while. He'd had Jeff trim his hair to a more manageable length, then he did the same to his beard. The mustache he had cultivated for two years was becoming a nuisance, so he cut it down to a stubble that matched his emerging beard.

Mabry had removed his shirt when there was a knock at the door.

What now?

He put his shirt back on and took his gun from its holster. He moved over to the side of the door and turned the key. "Come on in," he said.

"I'd like a word with you, mister. I just want to talk."

Mabry lowered his gun as the elderly man from the dining room stood before him. He was a thin man, bowed and stooped with age. The blue suit he wore was threadbare, and his white shirt had turned river-mud brown over the years. Mabry guessed he had to be at least seventy years of age. Mabry stood aside and motioned for the man to come in, then closed the door behind him.

The man held out his hand. "First of all, I want to thank you for what you did back at the dining room. Not everyone would've stood up to Rad Bascom and done what you did. That took some nerve."

Mabry shook the man's hand and noticed that it trembled as the man talked. "It's not my idea of being a good neighbor to see someone get run over for no reason." He went over to the desk and pulled out a cane-bottomed chair and placed it beside the bed. "Have a seat and tell me what's on your mind."

The man sat down and said, "My name is Raymond Alderdice. Most people around here call me Dice. I hung around outside the hotel after supper and saw you talking to Hank Garber. It was then I decided to look you up."

"I'm Frank," Mabry said. He sat on the edge of the bed as Dice talked. The old man's wrinkled face took on a reddish tint and his chin quivered. His hands never stopped moving as he spoke.

"I'll try to make it quick. Dave Harker over at the Slant-H is in bad health now. The ranch fell on bad times when Dave took sick. Dave went from a stout, robust man to a frail shadow of the old Dave. He kinda lost interest in the ranch after that. Rustlers saw their chance and helped themselves to Dave's stock. Then Hank Garber showed up a few months ago as Dave's new foreman and took over the running of the ranch. It appears Dave gave Garber a free hand with the ranch. Garber is a tough knot for certain. He brought three or four tough-looking men in, then booted several of the old hands off the ranch. He got the Slant-H turned around, I'll give him that."

"Did you know that Hank Garber offered me a job at the Slant-H?"

"I thought that mighta been on Garber's mind. That's why I came to see you. I thought you might be job hunting if you were talking to Garber. Hank Garber has plenty of hands over at the Slant-H and can do without you. A friend of mine has a big ranch about an hour outside of town who needs help in a bad way. The Bar-N has managed to hang on somehow. I don't know how much longer it can, the way things are shaping up. About all the Bar-N hands have left him. If you could see your way to lend them a hand, I know he'd appreciate it."

"Who owns the Bar-N?"

"A tough old man who used to be a Texas Ranger. A man named Samuel Peterson."

Captain Samuel Peterson?

CHAPTER NINETEEN

Samuel Everett Peterson had won a reputation of being a tough, no-nonsense fighter, proven by his actions on the battlefields of the Mexican War, the Civil War, and the Indian wars. Mabry knew this because he had served under Captain Peterson in Company K of the Texas Rangers. He had fond memories of that experience. He'd climbed through the ranks from private, to corporal, then to sergeant under Captain Peterson's leadership. All of that had happened before he had been appointed to the marshal's position. After leaving the Rangers, he had lost track of Peterson.

"Peterson bought the Bar-N about three years ago," Dice said. "Do you know him?"

Mabry shrugged. "I've heard of him."

"If you're looking for work, he needs hands and can use somebody like you. Nobody around here will sign on with the Bar-N because there's talk Peterson doesn't have the money to pay the hands he already has. I can't say you'd put money in your pocket, but I can guarantee that you'll have a good bed and plenty of chow. There's some around here who can't even find that and are too proud to say so. There were a couple of old Rangers who came along with Peterson who've stuck by him, and two old-timers. They need at least a dozen experienced men for that spread if they're going to survive."

Mabry thought the Bar-N might be the opening he needed. Signing on at the Bar-N would give him a base from which to operate and still maintain his drifting cowboy cover story. He knew he'd be among tough, able-bodied men if there were ex-Rangers on the ranch. And it would solve the problem of Jeff Keener having to prove he was a cowboy.

"How do I get to the Bar-N?" he asked, having made up his mind.

Dice stood with his hand on the door latch. "I saw Sara Peterson in town earlier at the dress shop. I'll get a message to her to meet you in the hotel lobby first thing in the morning. She can take you out there."

Little Sara. Now he knew why that gal on the veranda had looked so familiar.

CHAPTER TWENTY

The sun was shining through the lobby windows by the time Mabry descended the stairs the next morning. When he reached the lobby with his gear in hand, he saw Jeff sitting by the fireplace reading the *Carrsville Recorder*. Across the room sitting on a padded settee was the young woman he'd seen on the veranda the night before. The auburn hair, the blazing green eyes; yep, she was Hannah Peterson's daughter, Sara, all right. She had her mother's good looks and her father's air of sassiness.

As he got closer, Sara frowned and pointed a finger in his direction. "Are you ready to eat dinner, mister? I've got blisters at places where a woman shouldn't have blisters sitting around waiting on you. You shoulda been down here hours ago. If this is the way you work, I don't expect you'll be spending much time at the Bar-N. We don't cotton to loafers and laziness around our ranch. Now, if you're ready, let's get a move on."

Mabry smiled at her outburst. She had more than a little of both Samuel and Hannah in her blood. She was slender around the waist, and if she stood taller than five feet, three inches in her boots, he would've been surprised. She wore a tan, split riding skirt that reached down to her calves, a button-down-the-front blue blouse, and a brown leather vest. A tan Stetson hung behind her back.

"Wait a minute here," Mabry said, still smiling. "Who are you, and why're you passing out all these orders? I don't see a jeweled crown on top of your head. All I see up there is a tangled mess of red hair."

By then Jeff had joined him. He looked back and forth at the two of them as they exchanged words. He leaned in toward Mabry and whispered, "What's going on here? What's she talking about, waiting on you?"

"That miracle you prayed about last night came through. We're going to work for her father at the Bar-N."

"I didn't . . ."

Mabry held up his hand. "I'll explain later. Follow along with my lead and don't ask a bunch of questions." Mabry noticed that Jeff's eyes kept returning to the pretty little, freckle-faced girl who was giving him what for.

The man who had been behind the registration desk when he had first arrived came up to them and said, "Mr. Frank, don't you pay no attention to Sara Peterson. What she lacks in patience, tact, and good manners, she makes up for by being annoying and irritating."

"You mind your own business, Hubert. This lazy good-for-nothing decides to sleep all day and waste my time. We could've already been to the ranch by now."

Hubert laughed as he returned to the registration desk.

Sara looked over at Jeff. "I guess this is the other drifter Dice mentioned. At least he was down here ready to ride. That's more than I can say about you. He even saddled your horse for you. I guess he's become used to waiting on you hand and foot like a good servant should."

Mabry could see Sara was all stirred up, and she was blasting away at him with both barrels. He knew it was time for them to move on before she fired him on the spot—even before he was hired. "Hey, let's go if you're ready—time's a-wasting," he said.

As Mabry turned for the door, Hubert motioned to him. Mabry hesitated, then turned back toward the registration desk.

"Mr. Frank. I think you oughtta know something. Those three men you ran out of the dining room last night came by for their guns a little while ago."

Mabry nodded. "Thanks, Hubert. I'll keep an eye out for them."

When he reached the boardwalk Mabry could see the sun was well above the horizon. It looked as if Sara was right; maybe he had slept too long after all.

"What're you going to do about that Slant-H job?" Sara asked when they reached the horses. "The talk around town is you two agreed to go to work for Hank Garber."

"Yes," said Jeff. "What about it?"

They were right. In his excitement about seeing Captain Peterson again, Mabry had forgotten all about the job with Hank Garber. "Well, I guess I'd better drop by a saloon and leave a message. I expect one of his hands will show up sooner or later. What saloon do most of the Slant-H hands prefer?"

Sara shook her head. "That's not a smart thing to do. The Long Horn is the saloon of preference for their kind. It'll be filled with riffraff, thugs, and hooligans, even at this time of day. You'd be well advised to ride right past and let Hank Garber find out when you don't show up. Then again, it might not be a good idea to tell Garber anything, since you're probably going to be job hunting again tomorrow."

The three of them headed out of town, which took them right past the Long Horn. It was a little early in the morning for most of their customers, but as Sara had predicted, there was a motley crew of men lounging on the front steps. He noticed a couple of the men wore ragged gray uniform coats with gold braids on the sleeves. One man had the left sleeve of his Rebel coat pinned to this chest. Another ghostly-looking figure had a wooden crutch leaning against the wall next to a missing leg.

The men had a common look about them: abundant facial

hair, tattered clothes, and a gaunt, bony appearance. Mabry supposed they were out-of-work punchers, or disabled soldiers who couldn't work if work happened along. Over the years, he'd seen towns such as this filled with their kind. He'd never understood how they had survived from day to day.

But for the Grace of God.

Mabry rode over and stopped in front of the saloon. "Any of you gents work for the Slant-H?"

A grizzled old man with a cheek stuffed full of tobacco looked up and said, "Does it look like any of us here are working, mister?"

That brought a chorus of laugher from his friends. Even Mabry had to smile at his retort. "No, I guess not. If any of the Slant-H hands come around, tell them that the two men from the hotel have found a better offer and won't be working for them. Will you do that?"

The old man shot a stream of tobacco juice out into the dusty street and said, "Nope. I don't reckon I can do that."

Mabry leaned over in his saddle and rested his hands on the pommel. Why was this old-timer being so hard to get along with? "Do you mind telling me why?"

"Not a'tall. There's a couple men standing right over yonder across the street who work at the Slant-H from time to time. Why don't you go over there and tell them. Maybe they'll pass the word along to Garber."

The other men guffawed again and slapped the old man on the back. Mabry guessed there was a little humor in the situation somewhere, but he failed to see it. What he did see when he turned around were two men standing on the boardwalk, staring at him.

One of them was Rad Bascom.

CHAPTER TWENTY-ONE

Seeing as how he'd brought the subject up in a crowd, Mabry didn't see any way to waltz around it now. He turned Moses around and crossed the street to where Sara and Jeff sat on their mounts.

"You two ride up the street a ways and wait for me. I'll meet up with you later."

"And what if you aren't able to meet up with us later?" Sara asked. "From what Dice told me, I believe Rad Bascom's got a personal issue to settle with you."

"Jeff. You stay close to Sara. I know where this is headed. If I can't get the job done, both of you ride on to the Bar-N without me. And don't hang around."

Mabry remained still until the two of them rode a few yards away and stopped in front of the harness shop. He then rode over to where the two hard-cases stood. He wasn't so sure he liked the expression he saw on Bascom's face. Was it a grin?

He slung one of his legs across the saddle horn in a casual manner, pushed his hat back on his head, and said, "I'd like for you to tell Hank Garber that my partner and I won't be going to work at the Slant-H. We've decided to go to work at the Bar-N. If you'll pass along that message, I'd appreciate it."

"You'll come begging Garber for a job one of these days—if you live that long."

"Could be," Mabry said. "I've made my share of mistakes." He watched as Bascom's right hand lingered around his holstered gun. The wrist he'd hammered in the dining room didn't seem to be bothering Bascom any. The other man was one of the two who had been with Bascom in the dining room.

Rad Bascom sauntered out into the street and pointed a finger at him. "You made one hell of a mistake last night when you interfered in my business. I tole you we'd be meeting again. Now you git off that mule before I pull you off. I aim to teach you to mind yer own business."

"Do I have to tell your friend over there, too? Or is this just between the two of us?"

Bascom spoke to the second man, but didn't take his eyes off Mabry. "You keep outta this, Stoner. This is between him and me. I don't need no help."

The play was going about the way Mabry had expected it to go when he rode up to them. He dropped his leg down from the pommel and dismounted. He unbuckled his gun belt and placed it on top of the saddle. This was no time to start a shooting war in the middle of Carrsville. He rolled up the sleeves of his shirt and turned to face Bascom.

"Yer making another big mistake, Pilgrim."

"I repeat. I've made my share of 'em through the years."

CHAPTER TWENTY-TWO

A crowd had gathered around and had left a large open circle in the middle of the street. It appeared to Mabry this wasn't an uncommon occurrence in Carrsville. Bascom wore a smirk on his face as he handed his gun belt to Stoner. He spat into his hands, rubbed them together, and strode up to Mabry.

Mabry had a good idea of No Neck's plan; take this stocky, wide-shouldered drifter down with one quick, hard blow. If that didn't work, charge into him with fists flying. Mabry guessed the two of them were about equal in age and height: early forties, an inch below six feet tall, or thereabouts. He gave Bascom the edge in heft by about twenty pounds over his one-seventy. The trouble was, most of the difference seemed to be hard muscle. And worse, it had been a long while since Mabry had been in a knockdown, winner-take-all fistfight.

Mabry circled around Bascom for a few seconds, keeping out of the stocky man's range. Mabry threw a couple of punches that landed but did little damage. Then Bascom lowered his head, moved in closer, and threw a hard punch into Mabry's midsection. Mabry let out a gasp as he felt the jarring blow all the way up to his neck. Bascom followed up with a series of quick, hard punches to his head.

Mabry was hurt by the solid blows, and he knew it. Mabry heard Bascom let out with a loud laugh and heard several men in the crowd yelling for Bascom to move in and finish off the stranger. Mabry straightened up from the blows, dizzy, and disoriented. Bascom stood in front of him grinning, his arms hanging limp at his sides, as if he wasn't expecting a response. Mabry took in as much air as his lungs would allow and stood up in a flash. He slammed into Bascom with three hard punches to his jaw: right, left, right.

Bascom shook his head as blood seeped from the corner of his mouth. Mabry saw him wipe away the blood with the back of his hand. Then No Neck charged forward with a loud growl. Mabry spread his legs, and when Bascom got within his reach, he let go with a flurry of rapid punches. He saw Bascom stagger but keep his balance. Mabry backed away and took another deep breath. He felt himself tiring. He couldn't go at this much longer.

The two men traded punches for several more minutes with neither landing a solid blow. Mabry was looking for that one opening; the opening he knew would put Bascom on the ground. But he had to act fast or Bascom was going to wear him down. Bascom circled around and surprised Mabry with a solid blow under his chin that knocked the lawman backwards into a hitching rack.

Mabry felt himself stagger as he tried to straighten up. He hung on the rack with one arm and saw Bascom moving in on him. Mabry knew he couldn't take another blow like that. He slowly got to his feet and felt himself swaying as he tried to walk. From somewhere deep inside, Mabry called on all his strength and willpower to continue. He met Bascom's charge with his own punching fists. Hard, fast blows. Bascom appeared to be caught off balance at the flurry of punches Mabry was throwing. Bascom began to wobble on his feet.

Then Mabry saw his opening. Bascom straightened up with his fists hanging low. Mabry then connected with a right-handed punch to the side of Bascom's head. Mabry had put everything he had into the punch. If that blow didn't put No Neck down,

Mabry knew he would be in deep trouble. That was all he had left. Mabry fell to his knees and watched as Bascom's eyes rolled up in his head. No Neck staggered around in the circle as if drunk, then hit the dirt street flat on his face.

Mabry struggled to his feet and stumbled over to Bascom. He kicked him in the side. Bascom didn't move. At the same time, a shot rang out.

Mabry fell forward on his face in the street. There were no more shots. He lifted his head and saw Stoner clutching his right arm with blood seeping through his fingers. Stoner's six-gun was lying at his feet. Mabry turned as he heard a horse racing up the street behind him. It was Sara Peterson. She had a smoking rifle pointed at Stoner.

"You don't shoot a Bar-N hand in the back," she said. She swung the rifle around at the crowd in the street. "Any of you wanna give it a try?"

To Mabry's almighty relief, the crowd turned as one and drifted back to the Long Horn Saloon. He took his gun belt from the saddle, belted it around his waist, and climbed aboard Moses.

"Thanks, Sara," he said.

As he turned to ride away, Mabry's path was blocked by a man who carried a double-barreled shotgun across his chest. Mabry pulled hard on the reins to keep from hitting the man. He appeared to be in his late fifties, with a trimmed gray mustache. A thatch of gray hair poked out from the edges of his tan-colored, wide-brimmed hat. Mabry also saw that he had a badge pinned to his shirt.

"Leaving town?" the sheriff asked.

Mabry pulled Moses backwards a couple of steps to give himself more room. He leaned over in the saddle and said, "That was my intention, Sheriff. Unless you have other ideas."

The sheriff pointed toward Bascom, who was struggling to

his feet. "Might be a good idea to do that before Bascom can get his hands on a gun." He looked over at Sara and said, "Good shot, Sara. Amos over there said it was you who plugged Stoner. I'd say that shot of yours might've saved this man's life. I guess I can't fault you for that. I'll deal with Stoner and his misbegotten idea of manners."

The sheriff glanced at Jeff with a look Mabry would describe as scornful. "I guess we were all wondering why it was Sara who took that shot."

"I was kinda wondering about that, too, Sheriff."

Jeff's face reddened.

"Keener and I were going out to the Bar-N job hunting, Sheriff," Mabry said. "Sara here was taking us to see her father. Hank Garber had offered us a job at the Slant-H at the hotel last evening. I asked Bascom to take Garber a message that we declined his offer. Bascom had other ideas."

The sheriff stepped out of the way and said, "Be sure to tell Sam Peterson that Sheriff Vernon Tolliver said hello for me."

Mabry touched the brim of his hat, then tapped Moses with his spurs and rode down the street. Behind him, he could hear the grizzled old man who'd been sitting in front of the Long Horn hee-hawing like a lost donkey.

CHAPTER TWENTY-THREE

As they rode toward the Bar-N ranch, Mabry noticed that Sara was not as talkative as she had been earlier. He made a point to lag a few yards behind her, as did Jeff, whose head hung low. Mabry rode up beside the lieutenant and stared at the young man. After a few minutes, Mabry asked. "Want to talk about it? No sense sulking the rest of the day."

"What's there to talk about? I think I just proved you right about everything you said about me back in Dallas. I guess I didn't believe what you said about men out here not playing by the rules. I sat there on a horse oblivious to everything going on around me. I let you almost get killed because I hadn't listened to you back then. And of all things, a woman . . . a girl . . . had to do what I should've done."

"Sara has been around these kinds of men long enough to understand them. She saw the situation for what it was. You had been told what to watch for but ignored the signs. That's the very reason I had that argument with Reed Bannister back in Dallas."

Jeff appeared reluctant to look at Mabry as he talked. Mabry concluded the lad was embarrassed and had a need to clear the air between them. Mabry had similar feelings.

"I now understand what you were trying to make me think about in the dining room," Jeff said. "I got so caught up in watching what you were doing with Bascom, I forgot the most important thing."

"What is that important thing you forgot?"

"Watching out for my partner."

Mabry saw the serious look on Jeff's face. He thought the young lieutenant had gotten his first taste of the real world away from the big cities of the east: Boston, Washington, and Philadelphia. The part that worried Mabry most was the fact they were still at the beginning of their journey together. How would Jeff react tomorrow, or next week?

"I should send you straight back to Colonel Floyd for your own well-being," Mabry said. "If I had any sense, I'd do that."

They rode along for a while in silence. He could see Jeff was still beating himself up. Maybe, he thought, the young officer had learned a valuable lesson back there. The fly in the milk was that the lesson had almost cost Mabry his life.

Jeff slapped his horse and took off down the road.

Mabry put a hand to his jaw and massaged it, trying to ease the pain that shot through the left side of his face. His rib cage ached, his head ached, and as he took full inventory, he realized there were few parts of his battered body that didn't ache. Bascom was a hard-punching brawler, all right. Mabry knew he was fortunate to get out of the street with his head still attached.

I'm getting too old for these shenanigans.

After a few minutes, Mabry spurred Moses forward and caught up with Sara. "You saved my bacon back there, you know," he said.

"I wasn't shooting to kill Stoner. I just wanted everyone in town to know they need to leave Bar-N hands alone. We've got enough problems at the ranch without having to take time out for a burial service."

"Does that mean I've been signed on as a Bar-N hand?"

"Look, Frank. I don't know you, or anything at all about you." Then, nodding toward Jeff, who was riding up ahead of them, she said, "Him either. Watching you two though, I suspect you're the ramrod, and the greenhorn up there is along for the ride. He's got a lot to learn. I got doubts he'll last long enough to learn it all."

Mabry had to admire her ability to cut to the chase. Sara had them pegged after knowing them for less than a day. But then, that trait was in her blood, being the daughter of Samuel Peterson.

She continued. "As for you. I think you're nothing more than a hard-fighting drifter and a first-class troublemaker. Dice knew we needed help at the ranch, and being a friend of the family, he made his plea to you on a whim. The greenhorn up there came along with the package."

"He's a little green, that's for sure," Mabry said.

"It's clear you've got everything it takes to survive in this country: quick fists, a fast gun, and the courage to stand up for your beliefs. And you're a confident cuss, I'll say that about you. In less than twenty-four hours, you've had two fights with the man who is considered by most people as one of the toughest, meanest men around—and came out on top both times."

Sara was a hard one for him to read. He remembered her from the old days when he'd ridden alongside her father. At that time, Sam and Hannah Peterson had lived in La Grange, Texas, in a small house surrounded by a white picket fence with flower boxes hanging on the windowsills. Sara was their only child. He remembered how she had loved to listen to the tales her father told of his adventures. Mabry had visited the house a few times when Sara had been a youngster. She had been as rambunctious as any wild bucking bronco he'd ever encountered. Mabry wouldn't have recognized her now, all grown into womanhood, nor did it seem she connected him to those La Grange days long past. Mabry thought she would be right at nineteen years old now.

He looked at Jeff, whose head was still low on his chest. It could well be the first time Lieutenant Keener had ever considered himself a failure. And he was sure Jeff had caught enough of his and Sara's conversation to hear himself being referred to as a greenhorn.

Mabry was a little surprised that he'd begun to feel bad for the kid.

Chapter Twenty-Four

It was well past the noon hour by the time they reached the Bar-N ranch house. The ranch house was larger than Mabry had expected. The ranch itself appeared to be holding up well, even with the shortage of ranch hands. He could see a few indications here and there of recent neglect: a hanging barn door, broken corral poles, and a leaking water trough in front of the barn. Low priorities; chores that could be handled when the get-it-done-now work was completed.

They stopped in front of the house and tied off the horses to a hitching rail. Mabry looked around to see if any of his old Ranger friends were hanging around. He didn't see any of them. He did see a half a dozen horses in the corral, and a hundred or so head of cattle that milled around the buildings, grazing.

"Come on in," Sara said. "We might as well get this over with now. Dad might be at his desk, or might not be. Don't you be shocked if he sends you two on down the road."

"And don't you be shocked if he doesn't," Mabry replied. "He'll know a good man when he sees one."

"Huh," she grunted. "I'm a pretty good judge of ranch hands, and neither one of you stack up very high in my book. I'd be surprised to find out either one of you has ever worked on a cattle ranch."

She *was* a pretty good judge of ranch hands at that, he thought.

They entered the spacious front room. In the shadows at the

back of the room, Mabry saw the form of a person sitting at a desk. The man was bent over with a pencil in his right hand. He could tell from the man's profile that he was Captain Samuel Peterson. If nothing else, that hawk nose of his would give him away.

"Dad," Sara said. "I brought these two drifters from town. Mr. Alderdice told them we might have jobs for them. You'd better come in here and size them up before we turn them loose. Just so you know, the older one has already had two run-ins with Rad Bascom."

Peterson pushed away from the desk and moved over into the light of the room. "If he had two run-ins with Bascom and walked away from them, he must have something going for himself. Either that, or he's one very lucky so and so."

Mabry grinned as Peterson looked them over. Peterson squinted as he turned his attention back to Mabry and stared.

A smile creased the captain's lips as he said, "Mabry!"

Mabry laughed as Peterson grabbed him in a bear hug and swung him round and round. When he stopped his dance, Peterson pushed Mabry away and said, "Frank Mabry, you old coyote. Where in the world did you come from?"

"It's been a few years, Captain, that's for sure."

Peterson reached for Mabry's hand and yanked him closer to get a better look. "Frank Mabry," he said, again. "Well bless my ever loving soul. Lordy, lordy. How long has it been?"

Sara ran around to stand beside her father. "Would somebody tell me what's going on here? You two are acting like its old home week at the church social."

"Honey, this dirty-looking devil you brought home with you is our old friend, Frank Mabry. Sergeant Frank Mabry when he was with the Rangers."

"Frank Mabry," Sara said, her voice rising in anger. "Why didn't you tell me you knew Dad?"

"If you'll think back to the hotel lobby, Sara, you'll recall you didn't give me much of a chance to say anything."

Peterson nodded toward Jeff Keener. "And who's this young man you have with you?"

"Meet Jefferson Keener, Captain. I'll tell you all about us a little later."

Mabry pulled Jeff closer to Peterson. "Meet my former commander, Samuel Peterson."

Jeff shook hands with Peterson and said, "My pleasure, sir."

Mabry laid a hand on Peterson's arm. "Captain, I know it might be hard to keep it secret for long, but we want everyone around Carrsville to think of us as out-of-work drifters for a few days. Dice told me about the men who work here. Do you think you could persuade them to play along with us for a day or two?"

"I'm sure Sarge, Gil, and the rest of them will do anything you ask."

"Sarge came along with you? And Gil?"

"They were ready to give up the long days and hard rides, too. Two other old Bar-N hands, Earl Pickens and Rob Calhoun, have stuck with us through the bad times. It's been a tough run for all of us."

"That's the cream of the crop. You, Sarge, and Gil."

"And now you," Peterson said. "The two old-timers were pretty salty in their day, too, if you can believe the stories they tell."

He noticed Sara staring at him. She had something churning around in that pretty little head.

"Frank Mabry, huh," she said. She put a finger to her mouth, thinking, and then pointed it at him. "I think I remember you now. Didn't you always reach for the last piece of apple pie when you came to our house to visit?"

Mabry laughed. "That was me all right. Miss Hannah always

made the best apple pies in Texas. By the way, where is she?"

"Oh, she's around here somewhere," Peterson said. "She's always busy doing something or the other, whether it needs doing or not."

"Uh, Captain," Mabry said. "You might want to give Sara a commendation. She saved my life today."

"Well, now. How did my little girl manage to do that?"

He told Peterson about the street fight, and Sara's well-timed shot.

"I'd say she does," Peterson said, pride shining in his eyes. "I always knew teaching her to shoot a rifle would come in handy someday. Although I'll admit I had wolves, coyotes, and rattlesnakes more in mind than a man."

While he was relating the tale, out of the corner of his eye, Mabry saw Jeff turn away from them and walk to the door. He didn't know how long the young officer was going to pout. Mabry wasn't prepared to give him too much longer to put the incident behind him. The stakes were too high for both of them.

"Sara," Peterson said. "Why don't you take Jefferson out and show him around the ranch while Frank and I get reacquainted."

"Can't you think of another way to get rid of me besides that?"

"Go," Peterson said. "Show our guest some good Texas hospitality."

Jeff was still standing at the door. He glanced back at them with a solemn look plastered on his youthful face.

Sara marched toward the door without acknowledging Jeff's presence.

Jeff held open the door for her to pass through. She hesitated for a second, then marched through the opening, her back stiff, and her chin in the air. "Let's go, greenhorn," she said over her shoulder. "They want me to give you a guided tour of the ranch.

Make sure you don't hurt yourself while we're out there."

Mabry shook his head at the two young people.

Chapter Twenty-Five

Mabry and Captain Peterson sat in the parlor reliving old times. Peterson had flopped down in a soft chair that looked to be molded to his shape. Mabry had pulled over a smaller chair and had placed it in front of his old commander. Peterson wasn't a large man, standing maybe five feet, nine inches tall, with a slender waist, and narrow shoulders. He appeared to have aged beyond his fifty-five or so years since Mabry had last seen him. His face was drawn, his smile not so quick to appear.

While he was a small man in stature, his powerful personality and unmatched courage had made him seem much larger. Mabry had seen him back down many a man with nothing more than a stare from his steely gray eyes. He now appeared to have taken on the aura of a man fighting for his very survival.

"Dice says your ranch is seeing some hard times."

"I'm afraid so. We can hang on for another few months. Not much longer if something doesn't change with the cattle market. If not for the way we bought this ranch, we'd already be gone."

"What do you mean?"

"Hannah and I didn't have the money to buy the ranch outright. Sarge knew I wanted out of the Rangers, so he and Gil came to me and said they wanted out, too. The Austin politicians were making our lives miserable. And all of us were getting to the age that long rides and short rations were not as easy to handle as when we were young and adventurous. Among the three of us we managed to scrounge up enough money that a banker I knew agreed to lend us the remainder."

"All three of you are owners of the Bar-N now," Mabry said with a smile. "It's hard to imagine Sarge putting down roots long enough to take on the responsibilities of a ranch."

Then again, Mabry thought, he could have been referring to himself as well. Were he and Sarge that much alike? His brother, Woodrow, might think so.

"Hannah and I have the largest share of the ownership, which is right at sixty percent. Still, Sarge and Gil have done quite well with their portion. That is, up until the past few months. It takes all we've got in our reserve just to keep us fed now. And if something doesn't change, even that's going to be in jeopardy before long."

"What's behind your problems?"

Peterson shrugged. "All of the ranchers in the area have hit on tough times. We had a worse than normal winter. All of us lost a lot of stock to the weather. Then the market prices bottomed out. It would cost us more to make a drive to a railhead than we could recover with the low market prices. We're just sitting here, trying to wait it out and salvage what we can. We're better off holding on to the cattle and hoping for better days. We've all had to cut wherever we could. It was a tough decision to make—letting the regular hands go. We're down to a skeleton crew now taking care of a ranch that needs three times as many men as we have."

Mabry hadn't talked to Woody in over two months. He wondered how the Double-M was holding up. The saving grace was the Double-M wasn't near the size of Peterson's Bar-N. Still, a cattle ranch, regardless of its size, had to sell its cattle to survive.

"When the predators found out about the small crew, they came looking to pick up easy money by taking our stock," Peterson said. "We began losing cattle to those who don't want a job, but take what they can from those of us who do work. We've beat off a few of them, but they're making life tough for all the ranchers around here. We're all struggling to make ends meet."

"All of the ranchers?" Mabry asked.

"All except the Slant-H, I guess. They seem to be holding their own without much of a problem. I'd even say they appear to be prospering by the way they're throwing money around."

Mabry told Peterson about his conversation with Hank Garber in the dining room. "Hank Garber offered us jobs on the Slant-H ranch," Mabry said. "At higher than normal puncher wages. I got the idea that maybe he wasn't as interested in my cow-handling abilities, as in my gun."

"Could be. Dave Harker is in a bad way, from what I gather. I don't know the particulars, just rumors. I hear he stays indoors most of the time. He was always one who rode with his men and kept a sharp eye on his ranch. When his health got bad a few months ago, he took to his bed and let an old hand run the place. Wayne Crabtree had worked with Dave for years, but he wasn't the right man to run a large spread like the Slant-H. Before long, the ranch was in the same kind of trouble as the rest of ours were."

"Then Hank Garber came along," Mabry said. "Dice said Garber turned the place around."

Peterson nodded. "That's what happened. Dave allowed Hank Garber to do as he pleased with the ranch—and he made the best of the opportunity. It's almost like Dave had given up. Then this Garber comes along and turns the fortunes of the Slant-H around in a hurry. Not only that, he somehow managed to buy land around the Slant-H from those who had given up and wanted out. The rest of us couldn't afford to do anything but put food on the table and hope for better times."

"Has Garber given you any trouble?"

"No. He keeps close to the Slant-H. From what I hear, he's rarely seen in Carrsville. It's like he doesn't want to be seen. I'm surprised he came to see you at the hotel."

This whole situation was a mystery to Mabry. A stranger comes in, takes charge of a ranch, and turns its fortunes around within a few months. He does all this as the foreman—a hired man. And he keeps himself out of the public eye.

"What's Garber trying to accomplish?" Mabry asked. "If he's just the Slant-H foreman, what does he stand to gain by turning the Slant-H into a huge operation?"

Peterson shook his head. "Damned if I know." He leaned over in his chair toward Mabry and said, "And the way Garber's going about it takes a hefty amount of money. Dave always watched his pennies closely and wasn't a pauper by any means. But the way Garber's been operating the Slant-H, you'd think they owned the San Francisco mint."

"Hmmm," Mabry said. "That's an interesting statement."

"The Bar-N is stretched to the breaking point, and we won't be able to hold on much longer. We've got to find a cattle buyer who'll make a drive worth our time or we'll go under. On top of all that, there's a hefty mortgage payment coming due in a few weeks." Peterson waved a hand and said, "Enough about my problems. Tell me more what you and that young man are up to that sounds so mysterious."

Mabry and Peterson had a long history of sharing the most intimate details of their lives during their time together. Mabry would keep nothing hidden from his old commander.

"Jeff Keener and I are on what you might call an undercover job for the Secretary of War." He then related the story as told to him by Colonel Floyd in Dallas, leaving out nothing.

"You say that Colorado train robbery was about eight months ago?"

"Colonel Floyd said right at eight and a half months. I'll

admit real quick that the odds are stacked against us. The simple reason we're here is because of a piece of paper an army officer had on him when he was killed. The officer was trying to chase down the thieves when he was killed near Leighton. I found a piece of paper in the officer's shirt pocket that mentioned a place called Carrsville Landing."

Peterson put a hand to his mouth. After a moment, he said. "I don't think I've ever heard of a place called Carrsville Landing."

"Neither have we."

"Now that I think about it, Hank Garber showed up here around eight months ago. I doubt there's any connection to the robbery, but still . . ."

Chapter Twenty-Six

"That's the northern boundary of our range," Sara said, pointing toward a line of trees a quarter of a mile away. "There's a stream that flows through here year-round. I suppose you know that a dependable water source is critical to any cattle ranch."

"Oh, my," Jeff said, slapping his jaw. "That never occurred to me."

"Smart mouth," she said.

Sara had taken Jeff around the ranch and pointed out the barns, the bunkhouse, and all the work buildings scattered around the main house. She could tell by his reaction that he had never been on a big cattle ranch before—or probably a small one either.

While they were sitting on the ridge enjoying a cool breeze, Sara said, "I heard some of that conversation between Mabry and Dad. Neither of you are looking for jobs as ranch hands, are you?"

Jeff turned toward her. "You think I can't handle a bunch of dumb cows?"

"Well, yeah. That's exactly what I think. I think you're an eastern-bred greenhorn who's trying to look and act the part of a cowboy. It might be fun watching you make a fool out of yourself if you tried to ride a bronc or rope a longhorn. We haven't had much to laugh about around her for a long while. You might be good entertainment."

"You think you've got me all figured out, don't you?"

"Hmm, no. I don't have you *all* figured out yet, but I will. As you can tell, I've got a bad habit of speaking my mind. It's gotten me in hot water more times than I can count. And I can count pretty far. I'll let you know when I've got you pegged."

Jeff waved a hand to indicate the area that surrounded them. "This is pretty country, although it has a stark and barren look about it. The distant colors are vivid and beautiful. Have you lived here long?"

"About three years. Long enough to call it home. There's a lot about living on a ranch that I've yet to learn. I've got a lot of good teachers, which has helped. What about you? It's obvious you're new to this country, even though you look the part."

Jeff took off his hat and slapped it against his leg. "There you go again."

She smiled. "That greenhorn talk bothers you, doesn't it?"

He looked up at the bright blue sky and let out a huge sigh. "Yes, Sara," he said, a little louder than he'd intended. "I suppose it does bother me. I don't believe any man would like to have a pretty girl think him inept and useless."

"Oh, I don't think you're inept and useless at all. I just think you're trying hard to be something you're not."

Jeff was silent for a moment, then lowered his voice and said, "That was unforgivable of me back in Carrsville, wasn't it? It never occurred to me someone would try to shoot Mabry in the back, even though he had warned me it might happen. I was too naïve, or maybe I was too stubborn to listen to him."

"See? That proves my point. Out here you have to watch everyone all the time. This country is full of mean, tough people who will ride roughshod over you if you don't stand up for yourself, or for your partner."

"I let my partner down big time, didn't I?"

Sara nodded. "Yeah, you did."

They sat there in silence for several more minutes. Then Sara said, "You sound as if you're an educated man, Jeff." She was staring at him as he looked out at the country he had called stark and barren. "What're you doing out here in cattle country acting the part of an out-of-work cowboy? What are you and Mabry up to?"

Jeff spurred his horse and rode on ahead without answering her question.

Sara watched him ride away, wondering what big secret those two were hiding from her.

CHAPTER TWENTY-SEVEN

Hank Garber sat on his horse overlooking the Slant-H ranch. His neighbor, Hugh Fowler, was next to him sitting easy on his treasured Kentucky Thoroughbred. Garber could see thousands of longhorns scattered about the valley and near the low foothills to the north.

Fowler was a man who stood out in the territory. He was seldom seen not wearing a black business suit, a spotless hat, and highly polished boots. At sixty-two years of age, he had maintained his five feet, eleven inch, one-hundred-eighty-pound physique by taking daily rides around the countryside on his Thoroughbred, Zeus.

Fowler stood in the stirrups, shielded his eyes from the sun, and asked, "Are all those Slant-H cattle?"

"As far as you can see. And thousands more you can't see."

Garber didn't know a lot about his neighbor. He'd heard Fowler had bought his small ranch two years ago when he moved to Texas from Maryland. The rumor was the cramped city life back east had become too much for him after his wife's untimely death. He had begun to look for a different way to live out the remainder of his life. When an Austin friend told Fowler about the Whipsaw ranch being up for sale, he traveled west and investigated. Fowler liked what he saw and made Whip O'Conner an offer. The two men struck a deal within days, and Fowler became a gentleman rancher—on a small scale.

"The Slant-H seems to have survived the economic travails

rather well," Fowler said. "There are a lot of your neighbors who haven't been so fortunate."

"Your ranch seems to be holding on pretty well."

"I've kept my herd and my overhead small by design. My age and my financial status won't permit me to get in too deep. Besides, I'm not a rancher by birth like most of these men."

"I'll be the first to admit we've been lucky," Garber said. "When I signed on, the ranch was at the mercy of anyone who needed, or wanted, a longhorn or two. Dave wasn't able to stop them because of his failing health, and his ranch hands turned a blind eye at the rustlers, not wanting to confront them. Then the rustlers began getting bolder and bolder as time passed. Before long, they were running off hundreds at a time."

"Are you still losing cattle?"

Garber shrugged. "A few here and there, but we haven't been bothered on a large scale in quite a while. Like I said, we've been lucky. Have you lost many?"

"No, no. My range is much smaller, as is my herd. The rustlers haven't troubled me as far as I can tell." Fowler straightened up in the saddle and said, "I've taken up enough of your time, Hank. I'm just out exercising Zeus and trying to learn what I can about my neighbors. I'll drop in again one of these days."

Garber watched Fowler ride away and thought: you'd be surprised at what you might learn about your neighbors, Mr. Fowler. I don't know all your little secrets, and you don't know mine. We're not all what we seem to be sometimes.

Garber let out a loud laugh and spurred his horse toward the main house. "No sir-ree, Mr. Gentleman Rancher," he shouted. "You'd be mighty surprised if you knew everything about me."

Hank Garber entered the cabin that had once been the original Slant-H ranch house. The crudely built cabin had been constructed by Laird Harker when he and his wife arrived in 1842. It was a three-room cabin with a hard-packed dirt floor that was later covered with sawmill lumber. Laird made certain to provide a spacious loft for the children he had hoped would come along later. His son, Dave, had turned the cabin into the Slant-H foreman's quarters when the new, larger house had been built.

Garber slung his hat over into the corner. He dropped down in a chair and closed his eyes. A moment later, he felt a pair of soft hands caressing his temples. He let out a sigh, took hold of her hands, and pulled Lucy around where he could see her. "That's just what I needed," he said.

Garber released Lucy's hands and gazed into her bright hazel eyes. She sat down on the floor in front of him. Her hair was dusty-colored and cut short. She wore her hair short, she had told him, because she didn't like to waste time fooling with it. She had on a plain, white cotton dress with blue ribbons on its short, puffy sleeves. Basic, efficient, caring—and beautiful. That was Lucy.

"Where've you been?" she asked. "When you left the main house, I thought you were headed back here. I was waiting for you."

"I rode around the range for a few minutes. Then Hugh Fowler showed up on that big horse of his and wanted to look the place over. The two of us just wandered around for a while. How's Dave?"

"He's one tough old rooster, I'll say that for him. He might be around for a long time the way he's going."

Hank stood and pulled Lucy to her feet. He put his arms around her waist and said, "You keep a close eye on him. Don't let him go off and do something stupid—like talking too much. You can't forget why we're here."

Lucy took his arms off her waist and said, "Don't start with that again. We had an agreement about what each of us would do when we got here. You take care of your business and I'll see to Dave Harker. Together we'll get it done. We've got a plan, remember?"

She slapped him playfully on the cheek. "I repeat. You take care of your end of the bargain. I'll take care of mine." She then hurried out of the cabin and returned to the main house.

Garber dropped down in the chair again and closed his eyes.

My part of the bargain.

CHAPTER TWENTY-EIGHT

The eating area, which was large enough to seat twenty or more people, was rich with the aroma of Hannah's cooking when Mabry stepped in. It was located behind the kitchen with entrances from both the house and from the ranch yard. The strong whiff of Hannah's hot bread set his stomach to growling and his mouth to watering. Several loaves right out of the oven sat at the center of the table alongside a bowl of butter and a crock of honey.

Hannah had suggested that Mabry take the upstairs guest room while he was with them. He offered his thanks, but asked that she turn the guest room over to Jeff. Mabry said he'd prefer to take a bed in the bunkhouse with Sarge, Gil, and the others. It would be like old times listening to them yap at each other.

The large rectangular oak table was covered with Hannah's cooking: a platter of beef, a pot of beans, and a bowl holding some concoction that Mabry couldn't identify. But then, he'd learned long ago that hungry men didn't push aside anything when it came chow time. He looked around for an apple pie but didn't see one.

Sara was moving around the table pouring coffee and helping Hannah carry the dishes in from the kitchen. Captain Peterson sat at the head of the table while the others sat around the perimeter. Jeff Keener had dressed for supper, wearing a clean shirt, and spotless trousers. His hair was still damp and his face had a scrubbed look. Jeff had a seat to the left of Peterson.

There was an empty chair to Peterson's right. Mabry realized that he was late and took the empty chair when Peterson pointed to it. He found he was seated next to Russ Kavanaugh—Sarge.

"Welcome to the Bar-N, Sergeant Mabry," Sarge said. "We thought we was through with you long ago. I guess we was wrong. You're kinda like that bad penny we hear about."

Sarge had a swarthy, thick-chested look about him that made others take notice. It wasn't often you see a build on a man that would make a Brahma bull jealous.

Gilbert Alvarez sat across from him with a wide grin on his face. He nodded at Mabry, then resumed eating. Gil was the best horseman Mabry had ever seen. He rode like a Comanche and could shoot from horseback better than most men could shoot standing still. He and Mabry had been in several skirmishes together. Gil was one to ride the trail with.

After Mabry got himself seated, Peterson tapped his coffee cup with a spoon. "Sarge, you and Gil know Mabry from our Ranger days, so there's no point in telling you anything about him." He jerked a thumb toward Jeff Keener. "This young feller with him is Jefferson Keener. He says to call him Jeff. They're going to be hanging around the ranch for a few days. Sarge, you don't need to expect to get any work out of them around the ranch. They're here on other business."

"You didn't have to tell us that about Mabry," Gil said. "When did you ever see him do any work that didn't involve a gun?"

"Be nice, Gil," Mabry said. "My partner here doesn't need to know everything about me."

"He'll learn soon enough. All he'll have to do is pay attention."

"If anyone happens to ask you about Mabry and Jeff," Peterson said, "they'll just be another couple of hands around here for a few days." Peterson pointed down the table with his fork. "That's Earl Pickens over there next to Gil. And that fellow at the far end is Rob Calhoun. You can get acquainted with them later. Anyway men, Frank and Jeff are going to be with us for a few days. Help them any way you can."

"We gen'ly hit the range at daylight," Sarge said. "I 'spect I'll see you there since you'll be wanting to impress Jeff with your cow-punching ability."

CHAPTER TWENTY-NINE

Mabry led Moses out of his stall the following morning. He began laughing as the horse danced around in a playful manner. He nipped at Mabry's hand whenever he tried to pet him and pulled away when Mabry tried to throw a blanket over him. Moses was feeling his oats, not being cooperative at all. Mabry stepped back and let him have his fun.

"What are your plans for today?" Jeff asked.

After Moses calmed down, Mabry threw a saddle blanket and saddle on his back. He was tightening the cinch when he answered Jeff's question. "I have no plans as yet. I know I don't want to hang around the ranch any longer than necessary. Sarge would put us to work if he saw us loafing."

While they stood there talking, Captain Peterson joined them with a frown on his face. "Frank, let me take a gander at that piece of paper you found on the army officer."

Mabry pulled the paper out of his shirt pocket and handed it to Peterson.

Peterson looked at it for a moment, then said, "I thought about what you told me yesterday. I got what you might call a middle of the night revelation; one of those unexpected thoughts that comes to you when you wake up all of a sudden."

"I've had one a time or two. Then I'm always hard pressed to recall what it was all about the next morning."

Peterson stepped over to Mabry's side and held out the piece of paper. "Look at it real good."

Mabry did as Peterson requested. *Carrsville. Landing.*

"See that period between Carrsville and Landing?" Peterson asked.

"I see it. What about it?"

"I think that period means the army officer wasn't referring to a place called Carrsville Landing. I think he was referring to a place *and* a person."

Mabry looked at the paper again, then handed it to Jeff. "Take a look, Jeff."

"I think you're wanting to tell us more," Mabry said. "Don't keep us in suspense."

"Carrsville is the right place," Peterson said. "And the Landing part refers to Carrsville's banker, Avery Landing. Avery was a Union officer during the war and took over the bank from his father when he returned. I'd bet my boots that the army officer who was killed had been on his way to Carrsville to talk to Avery Landing."

"That makes all kinds of sense," Jeff said. "Stolen money. A bank. A former Union officer."

Mabry slapped Peterson on the shoulder. "Captain, you might have solved a mystery for us."

"Some things just don't change. I had to do it for twenty years for you boneheads."

Mabry turned to Jeff. "I guess we won't have to hide from Sarge after all. Get your horse saddled. We're going to Carrsville to do some banking."

"Do you think it's wise to go back to Carrsville in broad daylight after what happened with Bascom yesterday?"

"Perhaps not."

"You're going anyway?"

"Yep."

Chapter Thirty

When Mabry got within a mile of Carrsville, he pulled Moses to a stop. He turned in the saddle toward Jeff and said, "Captain Peterson said the bank was located on the south side of the street, next door to the hotel. He said there were no buildings behind the bank, just a wooded area that would give us a little cover."

"I take it that you don't plan to ride down the middle of Main Street?"

Mabry rolled his shoulders forward and backwards. They were still stiff, both from the punches thrown, and from the punches that had landed. He said, "I'll try to avoid it until it becomes necessary. But I doubt I can avoid it for too long."

Mabry clicked his tongue at Moses and pointed him off the road into a ravine where they rode for several minutes before climbing out onto flat, sandy ground. He eased up a slight rise that overlooked the town and stopped. He reached into his saddlebag and pulled out his binoculars. Mabry watched as several women scurried along on the boardwalk with baskets in the crooks of their arms doing their grocery shopping. To the east, a loaded freight wagon raised a low cloud of dust as it left town. A handful of children ran through the dusty streets, dodging horse riders and farm wagons.

It was a typical morning in a western town, he thought.

The hotel was easy to spot, as was the bank next door. Mabry pointed to his left down the ridge. "See that stand of cedar trees? We can leave our horses tied there and walk to the back of the bank."

"Tell me how you to plan to get the banker's attention. Look at us. Are you suggesting that two shabby, unkempt strangers like us go banging on the back door of a bank? That's a great way to get shot."

Mabry pursed his lips. "You're right. Maybe that's not such a good idea after all. Do you think we'd get a better reception if we strolled in through the front door?"

"Maybe."

When they reached the cedars trees, Mabry watched Jeff take off his gun belt and his battered hat. He placed them on the ground, then unbuckled his saddlebag and pulled out a clean shirt; the same one he had worn at the evening meal the previous night. He swapped shirts, then ran his hands through his sandy-colored hair and tugged at the tangles. He poured some water from his canteen onto a white handkerchief, which he used to scrub his face. After that, he slapped at his pants with his hat until they looked as presentable as current circumstances would allow.

Mabry was impressed. At the least, Jeff no longer had the look of a threatening bank robber.

"I'll go into the bank through the front door like any other customer. I'll ask to see Mr. Landing about opening an account. I'll then try to determine if this is a real lead, or a dead-end. You keep watch for us at the back door. If I think he's for real, I'll signal to you."

The young officer put his hands in his pockets after he gave Mabry a quick salute. He then walked toward Carrsville's main street whistling a lively tune.

CHAPTER THIRTY-ONE

Mabry stood behind a large red-trunked cedar tree as he watched the rear of the bank. He'd been standing there for twenty minutes or longer when he saw Jeff and another man appear at the rear door. Jeff waved at Mabry and motioned for him to join them.

"Frank Mabry," Landing said, extending his hand. "It's good to meet you."

Mabry judged the banker to be around forty-five years old. He was a tall man, well over six feet. If anyone had told him he was a banker, Mabry would have argued the point. The fair-haired man's clothing appeared more in keeping with a storekeeper's than a banker's. Right down to a white apron he had tied around his waist. The banker's brown eyes were bright and his wide smile was infectious.

Mabry pointed to the apron. "That's not the usual attire for the bankers I've done business with."

Landing grinned. "In a small town bank, a banker has to be the manager, the window washer, and the floor sweeper. I'm a man of many talents."

"I don't know what Jeff told you in the bank," Mabry said, getting right to the point of their visit. "We're here because of a mysterious piece of paper that was found on a dead army officer in Leighton."

"I heard about him," Landing said. "I never met the man,

but I was expecting him, or someone like him, to show up at the bank."

So they were on the right track after all. Captain Rainey was headed to Carrsville to see Landing when he was killed. "Jeff and I are in the dark about all this. Would you explain how you're tied in with the officer?"

"Let me go back a little, then maybe it'll make more sense to you. During the fighting around Richmond toward the end of the war, I served under General Jared Drummond. After the war ended, I returned to Carrsville where my father had managed the bank for years. I joined him at the bank and kept my Union views to myself as much as possible. About three weeks ago six gold coins showed up in the deposits made by the owner of the Long Horn Saloon. You have to understand that twenty-dollar gold coins are not unusual around here. But gold coins in mint condition such as those were are very unusual. The ones we see are usually dingy and well-worn from constant handling. I'd read about the train robbery in Colorado and became suspicious of what I'd discovered. I contacted Drummond and told him what I'd found. A few days later, I received a telegram from Drummond telling me I would be contacted by an officer who wanted to ask me a few questions."

Landing shrugged his shoulders. "That's it. That's the last I heard of it until now."

"Do you know who passed the currency at the saloon?"

"No. I didn't pursue it with Fanny Burch, the Long Horn owner. I thought it best to keep it to myself until Drummond could pass along the information for someone to check out. Since then, a few more of the coins have shown up at various places around town. The harness shop, the mercantile."

Mabry figured Drummond must have mentioned the coins to someone he knew in the army. The word then filtered down to Captain Rainey, who took it upon himself to investigate without telling the details to his superiors. Captain Rainey sounded a whole lot like Colonel Floyd by keeping information close to his chest. What did Floyd say back in Dallas? A secret is a secret when only one person knows it.

"You did right," Mabry said. "This might be the break we needed to round up those killers. Maybe we'll talk to this Fanny Burch after we leave here. Tell me a little about her."

"I don't know her all that well. I don't frequent the Long Horn Saloon. She came to Carrsville around two years ago and bought the saloon from Asa Morganfield. Morganfield ran a pretty clean joint back in the old days. He was getting on in years and had decided to sell. The Long Horn seems to be a gathering place for the rough crowd around Carrsville these days. It's not unusual to hear of fights and shootings taking place over there every few days. Another saloon on the other end of town caters to the quieter element. Fanny runs the place herself and does quite well from a financial standpoint."

"What about Fanny herself?"

"I'd say she's around thirty-five years old, maybe a year or so younger. She's an attractive woman. She comes across as a shrewd businesswoman with a quick mind. I've had a few business dealings with her here at the bank. She's always been courteous and has lived up to her banking commitments. I wish all my customers were as diligent with their financial affairs as Fanny."

"One more question then we'll let you get back to your work. What can you tell us about Hank Garber?"

"That man's a hard one to get a handle on."

"In what way?"

"It's common knowledge that the Slant-H had been having serious problems. Of course, all the ranches around here have been having trouble what with the hard winter and low prices. With Dave's health deteriorating, he began to spend less and less time overseeing the ranch's operation. His foreman at the time was an old hand who couldn't get the men to work like Dave expected. Before long, the ranch was just hanging on by a thread. Cattle went missing, and the ranch hands began spending more time in the saloons than they did on the range. All of us could see the ranch folding up right before our eyes. Dave's son, Clifford, never returned from the war, which made him even more despondent. We heard Clifford had been killed in Tennessee, or died in a prison camp somewhere. We never knew for sure. Then this Hank Garber shows up out of the blue."

"And things changed?"

Landing nodded. "In a hurry. Garber let the ranch hands know he was in charge right from the start. He booted a few of them off the place and replaced them with some tough, hard-nosed men he called in from out of town."

"Such as Rad Bascom?"

Landing shook his head. "No. Rad Bascom doesn't actually work full time at the Slant-H. During roundups and trail drives Bascom sometimes hires out. But he'd rather hang out in the saloons than work. There have been questions asked about how that bunch over there always has their pockets full of money with no jobs. Sheriff Tolliver hasn't been able to pin anything on them yet. He's still trying and hasn't given up hope."

"Do you think Garber is on the up and up with Harker? Dice told me there's a rumor about Harker making him part owner."

"Hard for me to say. I've heard the rumor, too, but I haven't seen any proof of it. No papers or title transfers have been filed as far as I know. Garber opened a business account here a few months ago and placed a substantial amount of money into the account. He's drawn on it to buy some of the land surrounding the Slant-H. Then he has made deposits back into the account whenever he makes a cattle sale. I can't say he's cheating Dave out of anything. Garber hasn't given us a lot to judge him by.

He only comes around when he has business in town to take care of. When he's finished with his business, he doesn't hang around."

They talked for another ten minutes, then Mabry and Jeff said their goodbyes.

"I think I need to have a talk with this Fanny Burch," Mabry said.

"You'd better hope Bascom's not hanging around the saloon."

CHAPTER THIRTY-TWO

After his conversation with the banker, a talk with Fanny Burch seemed to be the next logical move. Mabry hadn't intended to go to the Long Horn that morning and wasn't looking forward to a possible second encounter with Rad Bascom. Still, he had to do what he had to do. Jeff had gone to the telegraph office to send a message to Colonel Floyd. He told Mabry he would see him back at the ranch later that afternoon.

Mabry paused for a moment at the swinging batwing doors and surveyed the room. He breathed a sigh of relief when No Neck Bascom was nowhere to be seen. The saloon was loud, smoky, and dirty, like most of the customers he'd seen hanging around the place. There were perhaps less than a dozen men scattered about playing cards, or loafing over glasses of beer. Two bored saloon girls sat at a corner table away from the men. One was playing solitaire while the second one watched. A piano player pecked away at the keys of a piano at the far end of the room.

Mabry stepped up to the bar and nodded at the bartender. "I want to see Fanny Burch. Is she around?"

The bartender, with a toothpick hanging out of the corner of his mouth, nodded toward a solid wood door that had "Office" painted on it in gold letters. "You'll find her in there. Better knock first. Go in if she says to, otherwise don't."

"Good advice," Mabry said, as he turned toward the office.

119

He tapped on the office door and waited. He didn't have to wait long.

"Come on in," said a woman from the other side of the door. "It's unlocked."

The woman who sat behind the desk was beautiful, just as Landing had said. Her long black hair was pulled back behind her head and tied with a white ribbon. Her dark eyes were a perfect match for her dark, smooth complexion. She had a touch of rouge on her lips, and he noticed the slight scent of her perfume. For some reason, Cajun or Gypsy came to mind.

"Frank Mabry," Fanny said with a big grin as she watched him enter the office. "I wondered when you were going to drop by to say hello. You've created quite a stir around here since you arrived. But you have a reputation for doing that, I guess." She stood and held out her hand. "It's a pleasure to see you again."

Mabry didn't know what to say. He accepted her hand, more than a little baffled at her reaction.

"What brings you to backwater Carrsville, Texas, Mabry?"

Mabry realized that the drifting, out-of-work cowboy business just flew out the window with Fanny Burch's recognition. He found himself back to being Deputy Marshal Frank Mabry in a few short seconds. That didn't bother him too much since he was never comfortable playing games while wearing a badge. In his experience, pretending to be something he wasn't was a sure way to wind up carrying lead.

"Have we met before?" Mabry asked, after regaining a measure of composure. "I'm sure I would've remembered if we had. I seldom forget a beautiful woman."

"I didn't expect flattery from the rough and tumble Frank Mabry. But, yes, we've met. I'm not surprised you don't remember though. It was several years ago in Corinth, Texas. I was a young saloon girl feeling my way around in life. A drunken cowhand had been pestering me for some time. I didn't know how to handle drunks back in those days. You noticed what was going on and stayed close by me all evening. Then the drunk began badgering you for following us around. You ignored him as long as you could until the drunk decided you were becoming a nuisance. He made the mistake of drawing a gun on you."

Mabry nodded. "Ahh, yes. Corinth. You were wearing a red, low-cut dress with shiny sequins all over it, I believe. I think your hair might've been a shade or two lighter back then."

He could see the disbelief in her eyes as he related the details of that night. He'd always been able to recall incidents that ended up with him shooting someone. Those images stuck with him; they never left his mind.

"Yikes," she said. "And I thought I had a good memory."

Mabry smiled and said, "You remembered me, didn't you? Even with this scraggly beard."

"I recognized you yesterday, beard and all, when you whipped Rad Bascom in front of the saloon. Have a seat and tell me why you want to see me, and why you're dressed like a crummy cowpoke. That's not the Mabry I remember from way back. I remember a man who took pride in his appearance. If memory serves, you were even a little vain about it. And that long mustache is missing, too."

Mabry sat down in one of the visitors' chairs in front of her desk. There was no need to pretend now. He would ask his questions straight ahead in the open without trying to disguise his intentions.

"I'm interested in robberies and murder," he said. "You may have heard that I'm no longer with the Texas Rangers. I'm now a deputy marshal working this part of Texas. I'm investigating a Colorado train robbery that occurred several months ago. My investigation has led me here to Carrsville."

"For heaven's sake, a train robbery. What can I possibly have to do with a Colorado train robbery? I know my gambling tables have often been called into question, but I don't remember ever being accused of robbing a train."

"And I'm not accusing you of that, Fanny. I'm here because you deposited several bright, shiny twenty-dollar gold coins in the bank some time back. I'm trying to locate the source of those coins. Do you have any idea who might've left them with you?"

"I can't watch every game in the house at all times, Mabry. I'm not that good. We have a large crowd in here every night, and even larger ones on Saturday nights. This is my first venture into the business world, so I'm still feeling my way around. It's not as easy to run a saloon as I had thought it would be."

"Landing says you're doing fine."

"I'm learning. One of the things I learned early on is that things can get loud and rowdy in a hurry. I have a couple of men who keep things under control most of the time, but we don't have the luxury of being able to keep an eye on everyone who comes and goes. If we can keep someone from getting a knife stuck in him, or getting shot, I'm happy."

"Were there any strangers in the saloon that night? Maybe someone unusual. Different than your normal clientele?"

"As I said, Mabry, we have large crowds. If there were men as you described, I didn't notice them."

Mabry lowered his head. He'd probably gotten all the information from Fanny that he was likely to get. Still, he found himself not anxious to leave her company just yet. When he lifted his head, he could see her dark eyes staring at him, and she had a thoughtful expression on her face. He could feel his own face become flushed at her gaze. It had been a long time since he'd had a woman look at him like that. Or was it just his imagination running wild?

Fanny circled the desk and looked down at him. "I never had the chance to thank you for what you did back at Corinth. How about you joining me tonight for a home cooked meal? I'm not a New Orleans' chef by any means, but I'll come up with something worth our time. How about it?"

It wasn't his imagination running wild after all. He didn't have to think long about the offer. He stood and said, "When do you want me here?"

"Let's give ourselves plenty of time. How about seven o'clock, or thereabouts? I have an apartment right above the saloon. It's the one with the blue door. You can use the rear entrance if you wish."

"Seven o'clock," he said. "You can count on it."

Fanny thrust her hand under Mabry's arm and escorted him to the office door. "Don't you dare forget," she said. "I don't cook all that often. I wouldn't want it to be a wasted effort."

Mabry was pretty sure he'd remember. He hadn't had an offer that good in years.

Coy Dickson sat at a poker table holding a winning hand when he saw the stranger enter the Long Horn Saloon. There was something familiar about the man's walk, his build, the way he carried himself. Even though the man's beard covered much of his face, it came to him: Frank Mabry, the Deputy U.S. Marshal.

Dickson ducked his head and turned his face away from Mabry. Dickson had never encountered Mabry face to face, but he'd witnessed Mabry's tenacity firsthand on two different occasions. The first time, he'd watched as Mabry dropped Elias Sawyer with a lightning-quick draw in the Abilene stockyards. Mabry had been a Texas Ranger back then. The second time was when Dickson had been running with Cal Hardy's outfit. Mabry had caught up with them after a stage holdup at Shorty's Saloon in Coldwater. Dickson had been shocked when he saw the notorious gunman, Cal Hardy, toss his gun to the floor and surrender to Mabry like a whimpering pup. Dickson had managed to escape out the back door as Mabry cuffed the whining Cal Hardy.

What was a Deputy U.S. Marshal doing in Carrsville? Particularly one with a reputation like Mabry's. Was he here because of the rustling, or was it something bigger? No, not the rustling. He didn't think Mabry would be in Carrsville because the local ranchers had lost a few head of longhorns. It must be something else. And Dickson thought he knew what it was that brought him here. But how could Mabry know?

When Dickson saw Mabry go into Burch's office, he threw down his cards and headed to a door leading to a backroom of the saloon. Dickson stuck his head in the doorway of the room where four men sat at a table playing poker. The air was oppressive in the windowless room, and cigarette smoke was as thick as river fog. The mixture of soured sweaty clothes, whiskey, and unwashed bodies was enough to make him stop in the doorway.

"Porter," Dickson said, as he gestured for a tall, barrel-chested man to join him outside of the foul-smelling room. If there was ever a man who radiated evil, Dickson thought, it was Ike Porter. This particular job needed a man like Porter who rated money over scruples. If he couldn't get the job done, it would be no big loss to anyone. In fact, Dickson doubted anyone would notice him gone. Ike Porter had ridden with Dickson's gang for two years and had become an irritant. Dickson wanted Mabry out of the way, but if it happened to be Porter who came out second best, that wouldn't bother him either.

"I've got a job for you, Ike," Dickson said. "It'll take you and a couple more men to get it done right. Are you interested?"

"I'll be interested if you've got some extry cash on you. I'm running kinda low. The cards ain't falling my way."

Dickson reached into his jacket and pulled out a leather sack. He took out a handful of coins and handed them to Porter. "Forty dollars now, and forty more when you complete it."

"What about the other two?"

Dickson took out another forty dollars in coins. "Twenty for each of them. No more. I'm looking at you to get it done. When you finish the job, stay away from the saloon for a few days."

"Who you want killed?" Porter asked, with a loud harsh laugh.

Coy Dickson told him.

CHAPTER THIRTY-THREE

Mabry retraced his travel out of Carrsville by the back trails. He presumed Jeff was still at the telegraph office, or maybe already on the road to the ranch. A mile outside of town Mabry hit the main road where the travel became easier. While he rode along at an unhurried pace, he began to think about the conversations he'd had with Avery Landing and Fanny Burch.

Especially Fanny. He was disappointed she'd blown his cover right out of the gate on his first full day in town. On the other hand, he was delighted she had invited him over for a social visit. She was a beautiful, smart, enterprising woman. He was looking forward to spending an evening with her.

On a more serious note, he was certain it wouldn't take long for word to get around that a deputy marshal was in town asking questions. At least he could now ask them out in the open without trying to be clever and evasive. As for Avery Landing, he'd given Mabry every reason to think they were closing in on the killers. Who they were, and where he could find them, was a whole different problem.

One thing still nagged at him, however, and apparently it puzzled others as well. Why had Dave Harker turned the Slant-H ranch over to a relative stranger? Mabry decided to make it a priority to visit Harker and Garber in the next day or two and ask them face to face.

He tapped Moses on the neck and said, "Come on, boy, let's pick it up a little. You need some exercise." Mabry pushed him hard for a mile, then eased him back to a walk. "Good boy." Mabry then saw Moses' ears flicker. The horse slowed, and his head rolled from side to side, then up and down. Mabry lowered his hand to his gun and drew Moses to a stop. He looked in every direction, but saw no movement. Both sides of the road were covered with bramble bushes and thick scrub brush that could hide someone with ease. He was watchful and wary. Mabry nudged Moses forward slowly, his hand still resting on the butt of his Colt.

"What's the matter, boy?" Mabry said, leaning over and patting him on the neck. "What did you see? Did you hear something?" He moved Moses forward while scanning the terrain that surrounded him. Moses had sensed something. Of that he was certain. When he came to a sharp curve in the road, a man was blocking his path with a rifle pointing at him. Two more men with rifles climbed out from each side of the scrub brush, each with a rifle aimed at him.

They had him covered with rifles from three different directions. This didn't bode well, he thought. Mabry considered grabbing his gun and letting whatever would happen, happen. He was certain he could down one of them, maybe even two. For him to cut down all three as scattered as they were would be taking a big chance. With three rifles aimed at his chest, a shootout didn't seem to be a wise move at the moment.

"Come on, Ike. Shoot him and get it over with like we were paid to do," the man in the middle said.

Mabry looked over at the man who had spoken. He had a razor-thin face and deep-sunk beady eyes that seemed to dare Mabry to give him an excuse to pull the trigger. He'd seen that jumpy look on men before. The third man appeared to be of mixed blood. He had a dark, thick, stoic face. He wore a beat-up blue cavalry hat that had a feather stuck in the hatband. Mabry got a quick glimpse of him, then turned away when he heard the man in the middle talking again.

Mabry already regretted that he hadn't pulled his gun and had taken his chances. At that moment, he could have surprised them. He knew he'd lost that edge now and was at their mercy.

"What're you waiting on, Ike? Let's take care of him and get it done. Let's quit all this foolin' around."

"Shut up, Slim."

The tall, thick-chested man called Ike dismounted and strolled over to Mabry. He had a pockmarked face, protruding teeth that had turned yellow, and heavy-browed eyes. Worst of all, Mabry saw that the business end of Ike's rifle never left his midsection. Ike took Mabry's gun out of his holster and tossed it aside. "I'm goin' enjoy this, boys. I ain't goin' get in no hurry at all. I saw how this gent busted up old Bascom right good, and I aim to do the same to him. It ain't good for strangers to come in here whupping up on our citizens. Besides, I need some practice. I ain't had a good fight in a long time."

Ike smiled at Mabry, then threw a short sucker punch that caught him flush on the chin. Ike followed up with a backhanded slap across Mabry's face. Mabry felt himself hit the hard roadbed. He knew right then that Ike was going to use him for a punching bag.

He was groggy, his vision blurred. He tried to speak, but the words wouldn't come. The last thing he remembered was two men grabbing him by the arms and lifting him to his feet. They held him in front of Ike, who drew back his fist and threw a hard right fist at his head.

Mabry felt the blow, then everything went black.

CHAPTER THIRTY-FOUR

Coy Dickson dismounted at the rear of Junior's ranch house. He'd never been to the house, had only scouted it from a distance in case he needed to pay his old comrade-in-arms a serious visit. Spotting Mabry in Carrsville had set off warning bells he couldn't ignore. Dickson knew he could wait no longer to get his money and vamoose. He'd go to Denver, or maybe even California.

Dickson saw a man's shadow heading in his direction. A ranch hand. He ducked behind the corner of the house and waited until the ranch hand had disappeared before climbing the steps at the back door. He entered without knocking.

"Anybody home?" Dickson shouted.

In a moment, a man appeared in the doorway of the front room.

"Dickson. What're you doing here?" The man hurried to the front window and pulled the curtains closed. He then peeked around them. "What if you were seen? You could ruin everything."

Dickson noted the touch of panic in the man's voice. "We're in this together, remember?" Dickson said. "Aren't you going to offer me a chair? A drink? It's been a long while since we've had a chance to socialize together."

"You didn't answer my question, Dickson. What're you doing here? This is not according to our agreement. I told you I'd have the money for you next week." Junior glared at his visitor and added, "Although I shouldn't be surprised that you're here. You've never been one to honor agreements, have you?"

"Sometimes we have to modify our plans, old friend. Consider this one modified as of this minute."

Coy Dickson wandered around the room, taking in his surroundings. The ranch house was pleasant enough in a plain, rustic way. An old house. More of a cabin, he thought. He guessed he could live here if necessary. Dickson moved over to Junior and put both his hands on Junior's shoulders. "There seems to be a complication in our plan."

"What kind of complication are you talking about?"

"I don't know for sure. A marshal by the name of Frank Mabry is in Carrsville asking questions. He might've found out something about our adventure in Colorado, or he could be here for something else altogether. All I know for sure is Mabry is in Carrsville asking questions. And he ain't nobody to be messing with."

"You're certain it's a marshal?"

Dickson could see the concern written all over Junior's face. It might be best for him to put a bullet in his head and go on about his business. But he couldn't afford to do that just yet. He still didn't know where Junior had the money stashed. Dickson was confident he could force the money's hiding place out of Junior if need be—and he thought it might come to that down the road. With that marshal nosing around, he didn't think it would be a wise thing to do just yet. He would wait a little longer. He'd wait until Ike Porter solved their problem for them.

Dickson walked over to the window that overlooked the ranch yard and pulled the curtains open. After a moment of staring out into the distance, Dickson turned back to Junior and said, "I suggest you take double precautions from here on out. If the law has a whiff of the stolen money, they won't be sidetracked.

Especially since it's tied in with those soldiers' deaths. I'm moving our timetable for getting that hundred thousand dollars up. Three days, Junior. Three days."

Junior sat down and lowered his head behind his hands. *Why did I ever get involved with this maniac?*

CHAPTER THIRTY-FIVE

When Mabry regained consciousness, he felt water running off his face. Was it raining? He tried to open his eyes but neither of them would work. He began to twist around to ease the pain he felt in his side. His back hurt like sin when he moved. Then it was his ribs. Then his head.

As he became more aware, he started to feel sick to his stomach. He began dry heaving. The pain in his abdomen increased with each contraction. Then he heard a voice.

"Better take it easy. Be still."

His mind was spinning around. Again and again. He felt a soft cloth run across his face.

"He's coming to. Pour a little more of that water on this cloth. Let's get the blood off him and see what the damage might be."

It was a woman's voice. Not a young woman's voice; the voice of a soft-spoken older woman. Mabry tried to force his eyes open. They still wouldn't cooperate. He felt the soft cloth on his face again. Cool, reassuring. As he regained more of his wits about him, he realized that he hurt all over. And he began to remember why he hurt.

"We've got to get him to a doctor. He's hurt bad."

"Look at that face," the woman said. "It's swole up as big as a watermelon."

"I'll bring the wagon over and make a place for him while you tend to him."

Calling on all the strength he could manage, Mabry lifted a hand to his face and felt the soft swollen mass beneath his right eye. What about the other eye? He put his hand to his left eye and found it swollen shut, too. His mouth was filled with the salty taste of blood.

"Be still," the woman said. "Don't be so stubborn. Moving around won't do you a bit of good. We'll get you to a doctor as soon as we can make ready."

"Yes, ma'am," Mabry mumbled through bruised and split lips. He struggled to open his eyes, and after a few minutes, he managed to see a ray of light through a narrow slit in his left eye. He kept trying until he could make out shapes. He soon became disoriented with the effort he'd expended and gave up.

"We've got things all moved around and made room for him. I spread out the bedroll from his horse. It won't be a feather mattress, but I reckon it'll have to do. Let's get him loaded. I don't want to linger here. Those gents might decide to come back and finish what they started."

Mabry floated in and out of consciousness. He listened closely when lucid and picked up bits and pieces of what was going on around him. When they lifted him into the wagon, he felt his brain spinning out of control again, and he was gone once more.

CHAPTER THIRTY-SIX

The next time Mabry regained his senses, he saw iron bars through the slit in his left eye. He was in jail. His mind, fuzzy as it was, tried to reconstruct what had happened to him. He recalled the three men he had run into on the road, and the punches he'd taken.

With his teeth clenched, he managed to move his body until he was lying flat on his back, not so much on his right side. He kept working at opening his eyes. After a while, and lots of effort, the right eye opened enough that he could make out a few objects, although they were blurry and out of focus. Behind him, he heard a door open and footsteps approaching. Maybe he would get a few of his questions answered now.

"You decided to come back to us, did you? Doc and I had a bet on you. He gave me three to one odds for a dollar. I won three dollars by you staying alive. I told Doc that you were too tough to die from a mere pistol-whipping. I'll buy you a cup of coffee out of the winnings one of these days."

Mabry recognized the voice of Sheriff Vernon Tolliver.

"I don't remember much of what happened, Sheriff. I guess I would have to agree with what the doctor said: I'm surprised I'm still alive." He twisted around a bit more on his side, then asked, "Can you fill in the blanks for me? You can start by telling me how long I've been in jail—and why I'm in jail."

"You've been here for two days. You took an awful beating out on the road. That's after the earlier beating you had already taken from Rad Bascom in the street. The doctor says you were lucky to stay alive as long as you did. He said a man with less fortitude, whatever that means, would have died long ago."

"I'm not under arrest for anything?"

"Why do you think you might be under arrest?"

"I woke up in jail, for one thing. It's been my experience that people are put in jail for a reason."

"I don't know any reason why I'd have to arrest you. That is, unless you want to confess to some wrongdoing I don't know about. As to why you're in jail, well, Dr. Englehart asked me to house you here for a few days while you recuperated. He has a lady in his office bed about ready to give birth. She has run into a few complications and needs his full attention. She gets the bed, you get jail."

The sheriff pulled a three-legged stool up close to the bed and sat straddled on it while he talked. He had a roll-your-own hanging from his mouth. He struck a match on the sole of his boot and put the fire to the paper.

"This is a stupid question, I know," Tolliver said. "How're you feeling?"

"My head is beginning to clear a little. I remember a man blocking the trail when I came to a curve in the road. Then two more flanked me from the scrub brush. All three had rifles on me. I was dumb enough to walk right into their trap."

"Those men were the ones that did all the damage to you I'd imagine."

"I remember a little of it. One of them wanted to kill me right off; a man the others called Slim. He kept a rifle pointed at me the whole time. It was a tall man named Ike who was calling the shots. He wanted to have a little fun with me before they shot me."

"Ike Porter and Slim somebody. I don't know Slim's last name. He hangs around the Long Horn Saloon with that no-good bunch. I've had a few dealings with both of them. They never work at regular jobs, but always have plenty of gambling and drinking money. The two of them work harder to avoid work than they actually work."

"What stopped them from finishing me off? I have no doubt they intended to kill me. I heard Slim say they were paid to kill me."

"You got lucky. Your young friend came riding up and saw what was happening. According to his account, he pulled out his rifle and started throwing lead around like a wild man. He killed Smoky Joe, the half-breed, right off, and said he thought he mighta winged Slim. I sure misjudged that kid. He must've charged right at all three of 'em guns a-blazing. He said Slim and Ike took off in a hurry. Some kid."

Jeff!

Mabry stared at the ceiling as he tried to imagine what the sheriff had just told him. The young lieutenant had saved his life. More than that, he had done so against three hardened outlaws without hesitation.

"Don't call him a kid, Sheriff," Mabry said. "I think he's past that now."

"Then Onie Runnels and his wife, Clara, came along in their wagon. They were coming to town for supplies. They said they heard several shots fired ahead of them and stopped. Then they heard horses running in the other direction. They rode on down the road and found Keener bent over you. Clara and Keener were scared you were dead, but Onie was a war veteran and knew a little about death. He found you still had a little life left in you. They loaded you onto their wagon and Clara nursed you along until they got you to the doctor's office."

"Remind me to thank the Runnels when I get on my feet. If I get on my feet," Mabry added.

"Yeah, if those three hadn't come along when they did, you'd be playing a harp right about now."

Mabry tried to sit up.

Tolliver stuck out a hand to help. "Easy now, not too fast. You're not going anywhere."

When he was upright on the cot, Mabry felt much better. His head didn't seem quite as fuzzy, and his ribs preferred the new position better, too.

Tolliver stood and kicked away the stool. "I'm going across the street to get the doctor. While I'm out, I'll round you up a meal. You must be hungry. Make yourself at home while I'm gone."

CHAPTER THIRTY-SEVEN

Later, while he was working at opening his eyes, Mabry heard the steel door to the cell area open. He looked in that direction and saw Jeff and Sara. He squinted to better focus on his visitors. Sara's auburn hair was windblown and her freckled cheeks were rosy red. Jeff sat down on the sheriff's stool while Sara stood behind him.

"You look as though you've been through a meat grinder," Jeff said. "We've checked on you a time or two. We were scared you weren't going to come out of it. You took quite a beating."

"Yeah, yeah, I know. My pretty face is kinda messed up. Maybe it'll put some character in it when it heals."

Sara circled around Jeff, bent over, and stared at Mabry's swollen eyes. "You don't need any more character in that face. I just hope your eyes aren't damaged from those punches."

"I'll second that," Mabry said. "A man named Ike Porter is the one who put this beating on me. I'll find him somewhere along the way and give him a second go at it when there's no one holding my arms." He reached out and took Jeff's hand. "I understand from what Sheriff Tolliver told me, I've got you to thank for being alive. He said you came storming in guns a-blazing, or something like that. I'd say you've earned your spurs."

Sara jerked her head over at Jeff. "What did you have to do with it? I thought it was the Runnels who found him on the road."

"You don't know?" Mabry asked. "If I had the energy, I'd tell you. I think I'll leave that up to Jeff. Besides, he knows the whole story. I just know bits and pieces of it. If not for Jeff's quick thinking, I'd be a dead man, according to Sheriff Tolliver."

"Well, Jeff?" Sara asked, her hands on her hips. "You weren't going to tell me, were you? You were going to let me go on thinking you were a useless greenhorn?"

"We'll talk about it later if you want. Let's just say you and Mabry taught me a lesson about how a man should act out here in the Wild West."

Sara then turned toward Mabry with her hands still on her hips. "I want to know why this happened. Why did they try to kill you? This Ike Porter didn't just wake up that morning and decide to beat you half to death. There had to be a reason. And I know you two are keeping something from me. Let's hear it right now."

Mabry studied Sara for a moment, then said, "I think Lieutenant Keener can answer that question better than I can. Want to give it a try, Lieutenant?"

"Lieutenant?" Sara asked, her eyes wide. "Is he delirious and talking out of his head? Did he call you Lieutenant?"

"That's right, Sara," Jeff said, grinning. "My name is Julian Jefferson Keener. Don't laugh. It is Julian. Honest to God. Lieutenant Julian Jefferson Keener of the United States Army. Mabry and I are on a special assignment from the War Department. Our orders required us to keep our real identities unknown as long as possible. I'm an army officer and Mabry is a deputy marshal. My name wouldn't have raised any eyebrows around here, but we understood that Mabry had a well-known reputation from his days as a Texas Ranger. That's why we came to Carrsville looking like out-of-work drifters."

Jeff pulled at his shirt and said, "I don't make a habit of running around in clothes that look and smell this way."

"Well, that's a relief," Sara said. "It confirms my thoughts that you weren't a cowboy, anyway. I was right all along that you were an Easterner trying to act the part of a cowboy."

"Yes, Sara, you were right all along," Jeff said in a peeved tone. "Now you can pat yourself on the back for being such an astute observer. Give the girl a blue ribbon."

"Ah . . . look . . . I'm sorry. I was . . . well . . . rude, I guess." She stuck out her hand. "Now that I know the whole story, how about us starting all over again?"

Jeff took her hand. Mabry thought he held on to it a little longer than necessary.

"Yes," Jeff said, with a smile. "Let's start all over again."

"Now that we've got that outta the way, what am I supposed to call you? Lieutenant, Julian, or Jeff?"

"You can call me anything you wish except kid, or greenhorn. How's that?"

Mabry laughed in spite of the pain it caused him.

CHAPTER THIRTY-EIGHT

Sheriff Tolliver returned to Mabry's cell in the company of a short man with a potbelly, who wore wire-rimmed glasses, and carried a black medical bag. The doctor nodded his head at Jeff, then turned to Sara. "Hello, Sara. How's your mom and dad?"

"They're fine, Dr. Englehart, considering everything that's going on. They're both working too hard trying to save the ranch."

"Tell Samuel I'll be riding out that way in a day or two."

"He'll be pleased to see you," she said, as she turned to leave the room. "I'd better be on my way. I've got to pick up a few things at the mercantile for Mom. I'll see you back at the ranch, Frank." She then smiled at Keener and added, "And you, too, uh, Jeff."

"I see my patient has a little life left in him after all," Dr. Englehart said. "I guess you know if that gentleman over there hadn't come along, you wouldn't be with us. I had almost given up on you a time or two as it was."

"Sheriff Tolliver told me the story." Mabry looked over at Jeff and tried to smile. "He's a keeper, Doc." He saw Jeff's face redden at the comment.

"You cost me three dollars by hanging on, you did. That was a little inconsiderate of you if you want my opinion. I'll just add it to your bill to make it right."

"I'm glad you didn't give up, Doc."

Englehart reached into his bag and pulled out a stethoscope.

141

He hung it around his neck and said, "Let me give you a good going over, and then we'll see where we go from here."

Fifteen minutes later, Englehart backed away from the cot and said, "You're bruised and battered all over. Those men did a real job on you. But I can't see anything that time won't take care of. You might have a couple of cracked ribs. And that right eye concerns me as much as anything. We can put a tight wrap around the ribs and take care of them. After a few days, I would suggest you keep a cool cloth on both your eyes to help take the swelling out. I doubt that you get out of this without some scarring around the eyes and mouth. I'll do what I can to minimize the damage."

"You're the expert. I appreciate all your attention." Mabry reached into his pocket and pulled out a couple of bills. "Will this take care of your trouble—and your lost wager?"

"More than enough. Are you sure you can afford it? You shouldn't ride for several days in your condition. A cowpuncher who doesn't work doesn't get paid, you know. You can always pay me later."

"I'll make do."

After Dr. Englehart left, Sheriff Tolliver returned to Mabry's cell. "Doc said you can leave anytime you feel up to it. He also said you ought to stay off a horse for a few days. The bumping and jostling and all might not be so good for you. I can get word for Sam to send a wagon for you if you want."

"That's fine, Sheriff. Jeff here can handle that chore."

"Now that we've got all that settled, how about you two leveling with me?"

"What do you mean?"

"You know what I mean. The young drifter here sends a telegram to a Colonel Floyd in Dallas telling him he's in place. He tells him that things are proceeding as planned. In less than a week, you've had two bloody fights, and another near fight at the hotel. Then sweet little Sara Peterson has to shoot Jess Stoner to keep you alive. After all of that, your friend over here shoots Smoky Joe and Slim. It's almost more than I can keep track of all by myself. I'm thinking about putting on an extra deputy to trail along with you two just to keep score. I'll ask you again. What the hell is going on with you two?"

Mabry looked over at Jeff and said, "The cat's already out of the bag, Jeff. I was recognized by Fanny Burch over at the saloon from an incident that occurred years ago. We might as well tell him the whole story. There could be a time when we might need to call on him for help somewhere down the road."

Jeff said he couldn't think of a good reason not to tell the sheriff.

"Sheriff, my name is Frank Mabry. Most everybody neglects the Frank part and just calls me Mabry."

Tolliver raised his gray, bushy eyebrows at that admission. "Hmm, Mabry. That explains a lot right off the top. It's no surprise someone is trying to kill you. I suspect you've made a lot of enemies all around the state."

"I'm a deputy marshal these days, working with Reed Bannister out of the Dallas office. Jeff Keener here is an officer in the U.S. Army. We're on a special assignment from the War Department."

"This sounds serious," Tolliver said, pulling up the stool and sitting down. "Let's hear the whole story."

Mabry told Sheriff Tolliver what they were doing in Carrsville, and why. He held nothing back, including his suspicions that someone in the Carrsville area was involved in the Colorado theft and killings.

"Porter and those other two men came at me with orders to kill me," Mabry said. "I heard Slim say that plain as day. Someone around here must know why Lieutenant Keener and I are in Carrsville, or think they do. Whoever it is seems determined to prevent us from digging any deeper if they can. An army officer named Rainey was killed because he got too close to the truth. It appears we're closing in on the truth, too."

"Good Lord," Tolliver said, wiping his face with a bandana after he heard Mabry's explanation. "I knew something wasn't right around here, I just didn't have any idea what it was. I thought all I had to deal with were rustlers. Now you spring this on me."

Mabry struggled to get to his feet. Jeff hurried over to lend a hand.

"Sheriff," Mabry said. "We have very little to go on outside of a few new gold coins Landing found. Even that could be explained away somehow. But this attempt on my life makes me think someone around here is worried. Lieutenant Keener and I are going to operate out in the open now. If you have any thoughts, or hear anything that might help us, let us know. We'll be staying at the Bar-N ranch for a few more days."

Tolliver stood. "I'll be right back."

The sheriff returned after a few minutes and handed Mabry an envelope. "You might be interested in this."

Mabry opened the envelope and found a shiny twenty-dollar gold coin. He looked up at Tolliver.

"We found it in Smoky Joe's pocket," Tolliver said. "I think maybe you're right about someone not wanting you to dig any further."

"Here, Jeff," Mabry said. "You hold on to this coin. Someone might be able to identify it as part of the stolen currency."

"What are you planning to do next?" Tolliver asked.

"I'm going to try my best to get over that whipping Ike and his friends gave me," he said. "Then there are a couple of people I want to talk to." Mabry lowered himself back on the cot and closed his eyes. "Now, I think I'll rest for a bit."

CHAPTER THIRTY-NINE

The clanking of the cell door as it opened startled Mabry. He was lying on his right side facing the wall with his back to the door and couldn't see who had entered. He hadn't been asleep; he had been thinking about Carrsville—and why the killers had shown up in this small Texas cow town.

Mabry put his hands to the wall and tried to leverage himself over onto his back.

"Oh, stop that," Fanny Burch said. "You're going to wear yourself out."

She bent over him and used his blanket to gently roll him over. "There. How's that?"

"That's much better. Thanks."

"You're a real mess. You know that?"

"I kinda got that idea when Sara Peterson held a mirror in front of me this morning."

The swelling around his eyes had begun to diminish somewhat, which let him keep them open longer with less pain. His ribs still hurt, and his abdomen still had periodic spasms that caused him to lose his breath. Overall, he knew he was banged up and battered.

He took advantage of the improvement in his eyes as he gazed at Fanny. And there was nothing wrong with his nose, either. Her perfume was just the tonic he needed.

"I'm glad you came to see me, Fanny. You really are a sight for sore eyes."

Then she caught him by surprise as she bent over and kissed him on the cheek. She backed away and said, "I've been by half a dozen times to see you. This is the first time I've caught you awake."

"Well," he said. "Your visit is far better medicine than what the doc has been giving me."

Fanny moved over and sat at the foot of the bed. She cocked her head to the side and grinned as she said, "Mabry, I've experienced just about every excuse ever heard why somebody didn't show up like they had promised. I'll have to say this one tops them all, hands down. After all the trouble I took to cook for you, too."

Mabry smiled back at her. "I'd heard rumors about your cooking, Fanny. I thought I'd rather take a beating than to eat it. So I arranged with Ike Porter to get me out of that obligation."

She laughed. "You'll never know how much better off you are."

Mabry thought she had a nice laugh. Her wide, dark eyes laughed along with the rest of her face. "I might be persuaded to give it another try later. That is, if the offer's still open."

"It's always an open invitation for you." She then said, "For your information, Ike Porter and Slim Willis have both disappeared. They haven't been seen around the Long Horn since your friend and the Runnels hauled you in. It's good riddance to both of them as far as I'm concerned. The Long Horn will be better off without them stinking up the place."

Mabry twisted around again to ease the pain in his side. Then he put his right hand behind his head and lifted it up. "Do you think Hank Garber was behind this, Fanny?"

"I expect you're going to find this hard to believe, but I've never met this Hank Garber face to face. I've heard all the talk about him taking over the Slant-H, and about him buying out some of the smaller spreads. But I simply don't know the man and can't answer your question."

Fanny's comment wasn't what he'd expected to hear. That Garber didn't frequent the Long Horn like the other rough crowd surprised him.

Fanny stood. "It's getting late, Mabry. I've got work to attend to. I just wanted to check on you." She moved up beside him and said, "I've got an extra bed that's better than that contraption you're lying on now. Why don't you move over to my place for a few days?"

That was an interesting offer to say the least. Mabry gazed into her black eyes and knew he couldn't take her up on it. If he did, the distraction would sidetrack him from what he'd come to Carrsville to do. Afterwards—who knows?

"Fanny . . . uh . . . Not now."

She bent over and gave him another kiss on the cheek. "Remember. You've got an open invitation." Then she left.

Mabry watched her walk away and wondered if he'd just made a bad decision.

CHAPTER FORTY

Junior rode down the ridge toward the abandoned silver mine. He had a loaded packhorse trailing along closely behind him. The Adobe Hole Mine had been run for years as a four-man operation. The mineral output had never made any of the four rich, but it had provided them with a stake large enough to take them to California, where they knew they would make their fortune. What they left behind was a single, twisting mine shaft that penetrated three hundred yards into the side of the low hillside. Along the shaft were numerous narrow, low-ceiling offshoots.

A perfect hiding place. And convenient, since it was located a mile or so to the backside of his ranch. He'd learned of the mine from an engineer who had talked about reviving the operation, but had never received enough financial backing to give it a try.

Junior dismounted in front of a stone building that had once been the living quarters of the mine operators. And even though it had been left unattended for several years, the building was still a sound, solid structure. Junior tied off his mount to a rusted wheel cart that had once hauled the ore from the mine.

He entered the building and found a thin, pale one-armed man sitting in at a table with his gaze glued to a spread of playing cards. A nearly empty bottle of Killarney Irish Whiskey and a glass tumbler stained dark brown sat nearby.

Harlan Winters looked up when Junior entered. "At last," he

said. "I thought you were never going to get back." Winters lifted the whiskey bottle and shook it. "I'm down to my last draught."

"Who's winning?"

"I win about every fourth deal," Winters said. "Did you ever consider how hard it is for a one-armed man to shuffle a deck of cards?"

Junior laughed. "No. I don't think I've ever given it a thought."

Harlan then demonstrated his technique. "Whatta you think of that?"

"I think a man can learn to do most anything if he has enough time and enough determination." Junior knew Harlan had both the time and the determination. They had been together for several years in a variety of circumstances, and he knew all of Harlan Winters' strengths and weaknesses. And he knew Harlan wasn't overly pleased to be stuck out in the back of nowhere as a watchdog. Junior had promised him it would be for one year—no more.

Now Junior knew it would be sooner than he had promised, since he had confirmed Dickson's information about the marshal. And he had also learned that the marshal's young partner was none other than Judge Keener's son.

"Have you seen anyone snooping around lately?" Junior asked.

"A Kiowa family trudged by a few days ago dragging their belongings, that's all I've seen. I don't reckon there's a reason for anybody else to wander out this way." Winters jerked a thumb behind him and said, "There's a gang of rustlers hiding out behind those hills. I can hear them at night when they go on their raids, and I make myself scarce. They don't know about me being here."

"That gang of rustlers is run by none other than our old

friend, Coy Dickson," Junior said. "He showed up at the ranch and is demanding more money."

"Dickson? Here?" Winters asked.

Junior could detect the fear in Harlan's eyes and in his voice. Winters and Dickson had tangled before. Junior knew Dickson had not pressed their disagreement in Colorado due to Harlan's missing limb. Junior doubted it would make a difference to Dickson this time if Winters crossed him again.

"He's here, and he brought a marshal along with him."

"Dickson brought a marshal with him? Why would he do that?"

"Oh, not intentionally. You remember how Dickson likes to gamble. He left several of those new gold coins at a saloon, and they came to the attention of the town banker. The information was passed on up the line and now we have a marshal breathing down our necks. He's in the area asking questions about the coins. Dickson tried to have him killed, but Ike Porter couldn't get it done. We have to be careful how we deal with Dickson—and the marshal."

"I don't like this," Winters said. "I don't like it a'tall."

Junior knew learning that Coy Dickson was in the area had put Winters on edge. He'd try to calm him down and not let him get worked up into a frenzy. Winters was apt to act without thinking sometimes. Junior didn't have any special feelings for Winters, but he needed him around for another few days. After that, he couldn't care less what happened to him.

"Dickson and I talked it over, Harlan. Coy said he'd leave the country if I'd give him one hundred thousand dollars. I told him it would take me a week to make the arrangements. We'll see how it goes for a few days with this marshal snooping around. The marshal might solve our problem for us, who knows? If anyone comes snooping around, just tell them you've been hired to oversee the mine until the owners return. Just think, Harlan. In a few weeks you can go to Santa Fe and live in style like you always wanted."

"For fifty thousand dollars, I'll live like a king."

"Let's go unload your supplies, then I'll be going."

"You didn't forget that Irish whiskey, did you?"

"Of course not."

Junior untied the ropes and lowered the bundles to the ground. All told, there were four bundles holding flour, beans, cured bacon, coffee, tobacco, and other necessities to hold Harlan for another month. And, of course, four bottles of Killarney Irish Whiskey.

"You keep a close watch on things here," Junior said. "I'll take care of Dickson."

CHAPTER FORTY-ONE

Mabry sat in a chair on the porch of the Bar-N ranch drinking coffee. Hannah sat next to him humming an old hymn he'd heard in church as a youngster. He couldn't recall the title, but it sounded good the way Hannah hummed it. He thought back to those days when his father had been a brush arbor preacher back in the Tennessee hills, before they had given up their rocky hillside farm and had traveled west. His father had owned up to being a member of some obscure Baptist denomination, but he had always preached whatever came to mind after a night of Bible reading. He was being led by The Spirit, he explained.

His father had been led by the spirit to leave the Tennessee hills by stories he'd heard from a traveling drummer. The drummer had told his father about all the available land in a faraway place called Texas. After a night of fervent prayer, the Mabry family had loaded their rickety, mule-drawn wagon with their meager belongings, and had headed west the next morning.

As for Hannah Peterson, she hadn't changed all that much since the first time Mabry had met her. That must've been close to twenty years ago. She had kept herself trim, and was as attractive now as she had been back then. Her auburn hair was a little grayer now, and there were a few more wrinkles and worry lines around her green eyes. Mabry knew she'd been through worse times with Captain Peterson.

Mabry had returned to the Bar-N ranch the day after Fanny Burch had visited him in the jail. That was three days ago. The swelling had gone down around his eyes, leaving bluish bruise marks. His vision had improved each day, leading Mabry to think there was no lasting damage to his eyesight. The other parts of his body were coming around, too. One more day and he thought he would be back on his feet again.

"Did you talk Captain Peterson into retiring?" Mabry asked.

"Oh, no. I wouldn't do that to him," Hannah said. "I knew how he loved the adventure of the chase. There was a glow about him when you men gathered about him and took off after the Comanches, or the Kiowas. I couldn't take that away from him. It was his own idea to become a rancher."

"Do you think he misses being with the Rangers now?"

"Hmm, I think so. He's also quick to admit that he wouldn't be up to the hard travel and long rides as he once was. He knew it was time to do something else. When Dave Harker told him about this ranch, Samuel knew it was the right time and the right place. Samuel and the boys jumped in headfirst and made it a paying proposition from the very start. Then hard times hit us this year."

Mabry had thought Captain Peterson would never have ever left the Rangers. But then, he never thought he'd have left them either. The years he'd been a Ranger had been exciting and dangerous. But during those years they had put their lives on the line, the Austin politicians hadn't appreciated their efforts enough to see they got what had been promised to them. When Bannister approached him about the deputy marshal's job, he'd jumped at it.

Mabry and Hannah talked for another hour about life on the Bar-N, about his and Woody's ranch, and what the future might have in store for each of them. Then Sara called to Hannah and said it was time to start preparing the evening meal.

Mabry looked out into the distance and wondered what the next few days would hold for him. He'd already decided tomorrow morning he and Jeff were going to ride over to the Slant-H and have a talk with Dave Harker and Hank Garber. That itch needed to be scratched.

CHAPTER FORTY-TWO

Hank Garber sat in the office at the Slant-H ranch, his mind swirling with the rumors he'd been hearing. Too many of them were pointed directly at him. Could he survive all the turmoil that seemed to be swallowing the whole territory?

The original plan had seemed so simple. He and Lucy had covered every detail over and over. Now everything they had discussed was in jeopardy. People showing up he had not expected to see. A marshal asking questions.

Garber's attention turned toward the holstered gun that hung on a nail off to his right. The holster had cracks in the leather from lack of attention. He knew the revolver had suffered from the same inattention. He thought back and couldn't remember the last time he had fired that gun.

He went over and took the revolver from the holster. He checked the loads. The cylinders were empty. Would he have to use it again? As he was wrestling with his thoughts, he heard a knock on the front door. Garber glanced at the clock on the fireplace mantel. He realized he had let the time get away from him. He replaced the gun in its holster.

"Lucy," he shouted. "That's probably the banker, Avery Landing. Would you let him in? I'll get Dave and join you in the parlor." At Dave Harker's request, Garber had summoned Avery Landing to the ranch to discuss the ranch's financial situation.

Garber returned to the parlor a few minutes later with his arms around Dave's waist. "Careful, now," Garber said, as he led Dave over to his favorite chair and helped lower him onto the cushioned seat. Dave moved around to get himself in a comfortable position. Garber then pulled a chair up close to him.

Garber introduced Lucy to the banker. She then moved a chair to the other side of Dave and sat down. She sat with her back straight, her hands folded in her lap.

Hank could see Landing glance at Lucy with a questioning expression on his face. Garber put it down as the banker's surprise at seeing her. Since she'd been at the ranch, she'd had few opportunities to leave Dave's side long enough to get into Carrsville.

"Lucy, this is Avery Landing, the town banker," Garber said. "Avery, this is Lucy. She has been taking care of Dave for some time now." Garber leaned back in the chair and nodded at Dave. "This meeting was Dave's idea, so I'll let Dave do the talking."

"That's fine." Landing held out his hand to Dave. "It's good to see you again, Dave. It's been several months."

Dave coughed, then wiped his mouth with a handkerchief. "Avery, I want you to give me a rundown on the Slant-H financial condition. Don't leave anything out."

Landing opened his leather case and retrieved a folder of papers. He thumbed through them and got them in the order he wanted. "Let me say right away, without going into details, that the Slant-H has gotten through the past year remarkably well. The ranch's financial condition is strong, maybe stronger than it's been in three or four years. You still have one note at the bank in the amount of twelve thousand, six hundred and thirty dollars. All payments on that note have been made on time, and the initial principal has been lowered considerably. Furthermore, you have sufficient capital in your account to offset any emergency that might arise."

Harker reached out and patted Garber on the arm. "This

man has saved my ranch, Avery."

Landing then went into detail with the numbers. Garber could tell that Dave wasn't interested in the details and had stopped listening. Dave had heard Landing tell him what he'd wanted to hear. The ranch was in sound financial condition; his ranch was on solid footing.

"Would you like to look at the numbers?" Landing asked.

"Wouldn't do any good, Avery. I wouldn't understand them. You've told me what I wanted to know."

When Landing had finished his spiel, Dave said, "Avery. There's something I want you to take care of for me. You can handle the costs for this job out of my account."

"Of course, Dave. You name it."

"I want you to arrange with Neel Randolph to have the Slant-H ranch transferred out of my name into the name of Hank Garber. I want the lawyer to do whatever is necessary to make the whole transfer official. Everything goes into Hank's name."

"I expect Neel will have to know a few details, like the selling price."

"There is no selling price. I just want the transfer made, like I said."

Garber could see the banker was more than surprised. Landing was obviously shocked at what he'd heard Dave propose. Dave Harker was giving the Slant-H ranch, lock, stock, and barrel, to a man who had showed up eight months ago.

Landing looked around at all them. "Are you sure you want to do this, Dave? I mean . . . Hank has been here less than a year. To give him full ownership is a huge step to take. To sell it to him might be one thing, but to give the Slant-H away . . ."

"This is what I want Randolph to do. My mind is made up. Will you see to it?"

"Well . . . Dave . . . if that's what you want."

"That's what I want. Tell Randolph to get it done by the end of the week. If I need to sign anything, tell him to ride out at his convenience. I'm not going anywhere. I'll be here."

Hank Garber looked over at Lucy and winked. She remained perfectly still, but he could see a slight smile crease her lips.

Landing gathered up his papers and stuffed them back into his leather case. He shook Dave's hand and headed to the door.

Garber was waiting for the banker at the door and escorted him out to his buggy. "That old codger has a mind of his own, doesn't he, Landing?" Garber said. "When it's made up there's no changing it."

Landing climbed into the buggy seat. He picked up the reins and asked, "Did you know Dave was going to do this? Sign over the ranch to you?"

Garber nodded. "I knew."

"Did you try to talk him out of it?"

"No."

Garber was certain he saw a frown on the banker's face as he popped the whip and left the ranch.

No, mister banker. I did not try to talk Dave out of it.

CHAPTER FORTY-THREE

It was high time to put into action what he'd been thinking. Mabry told Jeff they were going to the Slant-H ranch to talk to Hank Garber and Dave Harker. He had waited long enough—too long.

"I once had a pet raccoon back in Boston," Jeff said. "You resemble him. And he was about as headstrong as you, too. Are you sure you know what you're doing?"

"Yep, I'm sure I know what I'm doing. What I'm not sure of, is whether it's a smart thing to do or not."

"I don't know that I wanted to hear you say that."

They had left the Bar-N after the morning meal. Mabry had explained to Jeff what he had in mind. He wasn't so sure the lieutenant agreed with him.

According to Captain Peterson, it would take them about an hour and a half to reach the front entrance of the Slant-H by the main trails. Peterson said they could ride across country and cut the time in half. Mabry shelved that idea since he planned to ride to the Slant-H in plain view of everyone. He had shaved off his beard and had Sara trim his hair back to its normal length. Then he'd put on a clean shirt and clean trousers. Last came his black vest with the marshal's badge.

Jeff had spruced up as well. The two of them were going to the Slant-H ranch as Deputy Marshal Frank Mabry and Lieutenant Jefferson Keener of the U.S. Army. Not as two job-hunting drifters. Then they would see what happened.

They had been riding for an hour or more when cattle branded with the Slant-H brand began to appear alongside the road. A few of them raised their heads, gave the two riders a bored look, and then returned to their grazing. A few others scampered away from them. After another half hour, they rode up to the ranch entrance where there was a gate with a bronze bell hanging between two ten-foot poles. A black lettered sign read, *No Trespassing. Ring Bell for Entry.* Mabry rode beneath the bell, which had a rope hanging to shoulder length. He tugged on the rope twice.

After a few minutes, Jeff pointed down the road. "Here come two men."

Mabry saw them, too. The man in front was an older man, heavy, with an easy way of riding. He carried a rifle across the saddle in front of him. He was smoking a cigarette and was staring at them through cold, gray eyes. The younger of the two wore a holstered gun tied down. He looked as though he was accustomed to wearing it. Mabry had not seen either of them before.

"We're not taking on any hands these days," the rifleman said. "You might try the Bar-N back down the trail a mite. I hear they're running short of men."

Mabry rode closer to him and said, "I want to speak with Hank Garber and Dave Harker. I have some business I need to discuss with them."

"What might that business be?"

"That's between them and me." Mabry pointed at the badge on his vest and said, "We didn't come here to argue, or to start a fight. We came here to talk."

"Give me your names. I'll pass them along and see if they have any interest in talking to you."

"Deputy Marshal Frank Mabry and Lieutenant Jefferson Keener."

Mabry saw the younger man jerk his head toward his partner at the names. He wasn't sure which name it was that got his attention: Mabry, or Lieutenant Keener. It could have been both.

"Go tell the boss, Billy. I'll wait here. You remember the names?"

"Yeah, I remember. Mabry and Lieutenant Something or the Other."

"Fine. Now go."

CHAPTER FORTY-FOUR

The man with the rifle hadn't spoken since the younger man rode away, nor had he taken his eyes off Mabry and Jeff all the while. When the younger hand returned, the two Slant-H men put their heads together and talked in low voices.

"Let's go," the older man said, as he motioned for Mabry and Jeff to follow him down the entrance to the ranch house. Mabry estimated it to be about a quarter of a mile ride. When he rode into the ranch yard, he saw Hank Garber sitting on the top rail of the breaking pen watching a bandy-legged bronco-buster earn his keep.

"Hang on, Arlie," Garber shouted, waving his gray hat over his head in encouragement.

"He'll never hold on," one of the Slant-H hands said. "That hoss is too much for him—or anyone." He let out with a loud shout as the buster held on for dear life. Mabry thought the ranch hand might be right. The big stallion might be too much for the buster.

About that time, Hank Garber let out a loud hoo-rah as Arlie went ass over eyeballs and landed with a thud on the hard-packed Texas ground. Arlie rolled over and struggled to his feet, holding on to his shoulder. The ranch hand who was cheering Arlie on jumped off the railing and coaxed the big black out of the breaking pen back into the larger corral at the back of the barn.

Garber jumped off the railing and strolled over to Mabry.

"The boys said you need to talk to me and Dave," he said. "Dave's not feeling too good these days, but I expect he won't mind having visitors." He pushed his gray hat back on his head and pointed at Mabry's badge. "I see you're not a couple of drifters looking for jobs after all."

Mabry shook his head. "Nope. My name is Frank Mabry. I'm a deputy marshal. My friend here is Lieutenant Jefferson Keener. He's an officer in the United States Army."

"Come on in the house and I'll look up Dave and see if he's able to talk to you."

Garber invited them to sit wherever they pleased. Mabry took a seat in a straight-backed chair. He didn't want to get caught in a soft, fluffy chair that might impede his movement. Jeff chose to sit in a straight-backed chair on the other side of the room. The kid was catching on fast.

The room was large, with lots of light coming in from two windows. The square-trimmed log walls were exposed and varnished, giving off a bright luster. All in all, Mabry thought it was a pleasant, comfortable parlor.

Garber returned with a thin, older man Mabry assumed was Dave Harker. Mabry had heard he was a sick man, yet for some reason, he'd had lingering doubts about the truth of the reports. Mabry had suspected all the talk of Harker's health might have been a clever ruse to keep the old rancher out of sight. After seeing Dave face to face, there was no longer any doubt in his mind. Dave Harker was a sick man. He was gaunt, pale, and unsteady on his feet. He had dark blotches underneath his eyes, and his pale indoor skin made the blotches all the more visible.

A woman was with them and had her hands around Harker's waist to steady him as they came into the room. Mabry hadn't heard of there being a woman on the ranch.

After they all were seated, Garber said, "Sheriff Tolliver has already dropped by asking questions about Ike Porter and Slim

Willis. Neither Dave nor I had anything to do with that attack on you out on the road. If that's why you're here, that's all I can say about it. It's true I've hired both Ike and Slim on occasion when we had cattle drives, but not for that."

Mabry thought there was a sincerity in his voice as he spoke of the incident. Still, that didn't mean he was innocent of everything else that was going on in the territory.

"Answer a question for me, Marshal. Why did you two think it necessary to come to Carrsville under false pretenses? Why did you lead me to believe you were ordinary out-of-work ranch hands at the hotel?"

Mabry shrugged. "We wanted to look around the area without being too obvious about it. We hadn't expected to get hired on our first day in town." Mabry nodded toward Jeff and said, "Lieutenant Keener and I are on an assignment for the Secretary of War in Washington. Our plan is to talk to all the ranchers in the Carrsville area. Since we'd already had a couple run-ins with men we thought were your ranch hands, we decided to start with you."

"Let's get on with it," Dave said. "What do you want to talk with us about?"

"Money, Mr. Harker. Around five hundred thousand dollars, to be exact." Mabry then gave them a brief account of the Colorado train robbery. He kept his eyes on Garber as he related the details. He thought he saw Garber give the woman a quick glance.

Dave shook his head. "And you think you can find a half million dollars out here in this windblown land of dirt, sand, and scrub brush?" Then he let out with a coarse, phlegmy laugh and added, "I want you to be sure to let me know when you find it. I'd love to get a glimpse of it."

"Not only money, Mr. Harker," Jeff said. "We're looking for killers as well. Three good men, and at least one not so good, have already lost their lives due to this incident."

Hank Garber sat up on the divan and said, "I'm sure I don't understand what all that has to do with us." He looked over at Dave. "Plain and simple, we sell cattle—when we can, that is. To be truthful, we haven't sold many recently. Indications are the market might be coming back, so we're holding out hope for the near future."

"According to the banker, we've been able to survive the bad times," Dave said. He nodded toward Garber and added, "Thanks to Hank."

"We don't want to wear you out, Mr. Harker. One more question and we'll be going. Your neighbors have mentioned the different quality of men you have working for you now. Especially since Garber arrived. The talk is they don't seem to be the typical brand of cowpunchers you had working here in years past. Is there a reason you let your old hands go and took on a rougher crowd?"

"I'll answer that if you don't mind, Dave," Garber said. "When Dave took sick, the Slant-H became the target of men who tried to rob Dave blind. I felt it was in the best interest of the ranch to hire men who could stand up to them and put a stop to the thefts. To be honest, Mabry, that's why I came to see you at the hotel. I can also tell you my way of handling the situation has worked. We no longer have to worry about losing our cattle. I told you we ran a tight operation, and I meant it."

Mabry looked over at Jeff and nodded. "We'll be going now. Thanks for your time. We can find our own way out. We might be back, might not."

Mabry heard Harker coughing and gasping as he and Jeff left the ranch house.

After Mabry and Keener had left the house, Lucy helped Dave up the stairs to his bedroom. She scurried around to make him comfortable and inquired if there was anything he needed.

He reached out a hand to her and said, "Lucy, you make me wish Ella and I had a daughter way back when times were better. And I'd want her to be just like you."

"Just think of me as your daughter, Mr. Harker. That would make me happy." Lucy patted him on the arm and left the room.

The view of the faraway hills had brought a calmness to Lucy. As she sat on the front porch of the main house, she was lost in her thoughts. She had taken up living quarters in the main house to stay close to Dave. Hank had moved into the nearby foreman's quarters. He'd said there would be fewer questions among the men with that arrangement. Lucy thought about her brief time at the ranch. Before coming to the ranch, she had always treasured her quiet time; reading her collection of books, or just sitting on the porch in the late afternoons as the sun disappeared behind the hills. Now things were different—much different. Maybe it had been a mistake for her to become involved with Hank's idea.

Lucy returned to the parlor where Hank sat on the divan. He had a worried look about him. Did he now have doubts, too? Had it all been a big mistake?

"How much longer are we going to continue with this charade, Hank?" Lucy asked. "When the word gets out about Dave signing over the ranch to you, there will be all kinds of questions asked. And now we have this lawman and army officer asking questions all around, too. That will only make things worse if they find out what you're up to."

Hank patted the divan and motioned her over to sit beside him. He put his arm around her shoulder and pulled her close. "I know, I know," he said. "But we've gone too far with this to stop now. We can still make it work. In fact, the marshal showing up might help us."

"Hank, you have to come to grips with the past. We both

know it wasn't you who made all those decisions. Sure, you were a big part of it, but you weren't alone."

"But I benefitted by the decisions. I'm not sure how the people will accept my explanation."

She felt a chill run along her spine. Lucy was certain their lives were about to change with this Mabry poking his nose around. Would it change for the better, or for the worse?

CHAPTER FORTY-FIVE

Captain Peterson was seated in the main room smoking a pipe when Mabry returned to the Bar-N. Peterson had his legs crossed, with his feet resting on a cushioned ottoman. A glass of tea sat on a table by his side.

"I see you're hard at it today," Mabry said.

"Have been. It's my afternoon break. You'll be looking forward to a break yourself one of these days."

"I hope you're right, Captain."

"I see you two made it back from the Slant-H with all your body parts intact. I'll have to say I was a little worried about you." He put his feet to the floor, leaned over, and said, "So, tell me about it. Did you see Dave? Get to talk to him?"

"Yes, we saw Dave and talked to him, but I'm not sure what to make of our conversation. We let both Dave and Hank Garber know who we are, and why we're in the Carrsville area. We talked for a few minutes, but didn't learn a lot. Neither Dave nor Garber seemed too worried about our being around asking questions."

"Dave appeared to be in bad shape physically," Jeff said. "I don't know that he's got a lot of time left. And he had a lady there who has been taking care of him. Did you know that?"

Peterson lifted his eyebrows. "A lady taking care of Dave? No. I'd never heard that. I'll have to give that some thought."

"She was a nice-looking woman," Mabry said. "Mid-thirties, early forties. Short hair. She sat beside Dave the whole time and

168

didn't say a word."

"If Hank Garber was out to hornswoggle Dave and steal his ranch, why would he have someone there to take care of him? That doesn't make a lot of sense. I really ought to go talk to him. Every time I've tried in the past, I was given some excuse why I couldn't see him. At the time, I thought Garber was just making excuses because he didn't want Dave talking to me. Now, after listening to you, I don't know what to think. I just know I've got to go over there again—and soon."

Mabry smiled at Peterson and said, "Maybe I'm a real sucker, but Garber even convinced me he had nothing to do with the whipping Porter and Slim gave me. To be truthful, our visit raised more questions in my mind than it answered."

"Well, I'm going over there to see Dave if I have to shoot my way in. Maybe tomorrow."

Mabry knew better than to try to argue with him. When that man made up his mind, there was no changing it. Besides, Mabry wasn't so sure he wanted to change the captain's mind. Peterson might be able to find out more from Dave than he had.

"You do that," Mabry said. "I'm going back to Carrsville to nose around a little." He looked over at Jeff. "You stay close by and watch out for things here while I'm out and about. I might be back tonight, might not."

Mabry didn't see any need for Jeff tagging along with him. And while he was in Carrsville, he just might stop by to see what's going on at the Long Horn. What did Fanny say to him? Always an open invitation? Blue door?

CHAPTER FORTY-SIX

Frank Mabry marched in the front door of the Long Horn, his eyes wary and challenging. If anyone had any objections to him being there, he was ready to accommodate them. He'd been in this little hamlet long enough. He was ready to finish this business and move on.

There were a few men lounging around. Mabry didn't spot anyone who seemed to pay special attention to him. Fanny was nowhere to be seen. It was early afternoon, so maybe she was in her office.

The toothpick-chewing bartender noticed him looking around and jerked his head up toward the stairs. "Top of the stairs. Blue door. Same as last time. Knock first. She said you might be dropping by."

Mabry nodded his thanks and headed for the stairs. The blue door was the first door on the right. There were three other doors down the narrow hallway, each painted a different color.

He rapped on the door with his knuckles and said, "It's Mabry."

Fanny opened the door and stood there with a bright smile on her face. Before she could say anything, he moved past her into the room. He heard the door close behind him. He tossed his hat on a chair and turned to face her. She had on a thin, light-blue dressing gown that brought out the darkness of her eyes and her skin—and gave him a hint of her other assets. Her hair was damp, as if she had just washed it.

"I'd about given up on you," she said. "I thought you had forgotten about my open invitation."

He shook his head. "Nope. I never forgot. I just had to get my strength built up."

She let out a little giggle, rushed over to him, and threw her arms around his neck. He stared at her for a moment, then let nature take its course.

Later, as they lay side by side on her oversized bed, Fanny said, "I hear you're still stirring up trouble. The talk is you have the Slant-H ranch in your gunsight now. What is it about you that trouble tags along everywhere you go?"

"That's my lot in life, Fanny. If I don't run across any turmoil by noontime, I feel like it's my duty to create some."

"I've noticed that trait always seems to follow certain men. In the saloon business, for instance, the same men seem to create the most problems for me day after day. Others just as tough can go forever without causing a fuss. I've never understood it."

"It's because a few of us are always sticking our noses in other people's business. At least that's what I've been told about a hundred times."

She had a deep, throaty laugh, and let it flow. "It's as good an explanation as I've heard. I've kept my ears open for you, Mabry. Everyone's talking about you showing up here out of the blue. They're all speculating about who you're after. So tell me. Have you made any progress in locating the stolen money and the thieves?"

"Nope. None at all."

She lifted herself up on her elbows and stared at him. "Does that mean you're going to be leaving soon? Chasing down a lead somewhere else?"

He turned toward her, placed his hands around her questioning face, and said, "It actually means I'm gonna have to stick around here a little longer until I'm certain this lead is a dead-end. You're not getting rid of me that easy."

She pressed his hands tight to her face. "That's what I wanted to hear you say." She leaned over and gave him a lingering kiss, then climbed out of the bed. "You can stay here or leave. Your choice. My choice is you stay, but I know you've got a load of things on your mind. Right now I've got to get downstairs. This saloon won't run itself."

Mabry stayed in the room until Fanny left, then he departed by the rear exit. He was pretty sure he'd be back.

Rad Bascom stood in the shadows of the building adjacent to the Long Horn Saloon. The gossipy bartender had openly talked about Mabry spending the afternoon upstairs with Fanny. When Bascom saw Fanny descend the stairway inside the saloon, he hurried through the batwing doors to a spot where he could see the rear entrance. He was going to get even with Mabry for that whipping out in the street.

Bascom had never knowingly killed a man, although he had come close a time or two with his fists. During the war, he had served in an artillery battery that had bombarded Yankee troops mercilessly on several occasions. But that was different than killing a man face to face. Still, he had to do it. Every time he thought about the whipping, he became angrier and angrier. And the cowpokes and rowdies in the saloon hadn't paid him near enough respect since that fight. He'd heard the whispers and the laughs.

Bascom had smoked two cigarettes before Mabry emerged from the saloon. He watched as the marshal tugged at his gun belt, straightened his hat, and scanned his surroundings.

He's being cautious, Bascom thought.

Bascom lifted his gun from his holster and waited. Mabry was too far away for a certain kill shot. He'd never been as good with a handgun as he'd led people to believe. But the marshal had to walk in his direction to get to his horse. He'd let the marshal come to him; let him walk into his own death. He continued to watch as Mabry turned away from the rear of the saloon and headed toward the boardwalk. Bascom took aim.

Just as he was about to pull the trigger, Bascom heard someone say, "Mabry. Just the man I've been looking for. There's a couple things we need to talk about."

It was the banker, Avery Landing.

"Let me round up my horse," Mabry said. "I'll be over to see you in a few minutes."

Bascom retreated back into the shadows of the building. He looked down at his hands. They were trembling. He was so close to getting even with Mabry.

As Mabry climbed into his saddle, Bascom heard the marshal say, "Too bad the banker came along, Bascom. You were about ten seconds away from meeting your maker. I'd get outta Carrsville as fast as a horse could take me if I was in your boots. The next time I see you, we'll be throwing lead at each other. And if you'll ask around, you'll find I seldom miss."

No Neck Bascom shoved his gun into his holster and ran down the street without looking back.

CHAPTER FORTY-SEVEN

The deputy marshal strolled through the bank as if he were a wealthy customer dying to place a hunk of his change in the loving care of Avery Landing. He was wearing his black vest with the marshal's badge displayed in plain sight. He had visited the general store earlier and had bought a new blue shirt with pearl-like buttons, a new red bandana, and new denim pants. All with army money. When he thought about it, he had returned to the store and bought a new gray Stetson and tossed his old hat in the trash can.

Mabry was sure the word had already spread that a marshal was in town making a nuisance of himself. He had decided to look the part.

A young man stood behind the teller's window counting out banknotes to a man. He glanced at Mabry and said, "Be with you in a moment." Mabry saw that Avery Landing's office door was open so he bypassed the teller and went directly to the office. He found Landing staring out the window as if in a trance.

"What's got your attention out there?" Mabry asked. "Did you spot a fox in that clump of cedar trees?"

Landing spun around in his chair and put a hand over his heart. "Mabry! Don't slip up on me like that. Make a little noise, for heaven's sake."

Mabry laughed. "It's just the old lawman in me coming out." He sat down in a visitor's chair across from the banker's polished oak desk. The office wasn't ornate by any means. It had all the necessities: two file cabinets, a black safe with a dial combination lock, and a tall gun cabinet that held a shotgun and a rifle. Mabry picked up a framed photograph of Landing and an attractive woman. Two young girls sat between them.

"Nice-looking family," Mabry said, then replaced the picture on the desk. "I hope to have a family myself one of these days."

Landing came around the desk and shut the office door. Instead of returning to the chair behind his desk, Landing sat in a chair close to the marshal. "Marshal," he said in a low, conspiratorial tone. "I found out something about the Slant-H that bothers me. I realize I shouldn't say anything to you about it. I'm probably breaking a dozen banking regulations by telling you this. But given what I know about your investigation, I wouldn't feel right keeping it from you."

"I'm listening, and the regulators will never get me to admit you ever told me anything. There. Does that ease your mind?"

"No, but I'm going to tell you anyway. Knowing that Neel Randolph is a drunken old gossip makes it easier. Everybody in town will know by sundown, if they don't already. The news is too big for Neel not to tell. Dave Harker has asked Randolph—he's the town's only lawyer—to draw up papers to turn the Slant-H over to Hank Garber."

"Garber is buying the Slant-H?"

Landing shook his head. "No. Not buying. Dave is *giving* the ranch to Garber. I suspect Randolph will require a token amount of money to change hands to make it legal. Can you imagine this happening? Dave Harker is making a gift of the Slant-H ranch to Hank Garber."

Mabry sat back and tried to digest the information. While he'd been surprised at the somewhat pleasant atmosphere he'd found on his trip to the Slant-H, he'd never dreamed of Harker making Garber a present of the ranch. That didn't sound right.

"That's a real shocker, Avery," Mabry said.

"Dave asked me to put Randolph to work on it and to have it finished by the end of the week. That's two days away. Hank Garber knew Dave was going to do this, too. When I asked Garber if he'd tried to talk Dave out of making this deed transfer, Garber just smiled at me and said, 'No.' "

"It's almost like this was what Garber was working toward from the get-go," Mabry said. "Thanks for the information, Avery. I'll keep it to myself until I hear it from someone else. It's fair game if I hear it again."

Mabry stood on the boardwalk and glanced around the town as he thought about Hank Garber. It seemed the foreman had wormed his way into Harker's affections by turning around the ranch's fortunes. But to hand the ranch over to Garber outright seemed to be overdoing his thanks.

CHAPTER FORTY-EIGHT

There were a few clouds gathering to the north, and Mabry thought he could hear a faraway rumble or two. The sparse grass around the ranches could certainly use a wetting. But it was more than likely wishful thinking. He had left the Carrsville Hotel well past sunrise after he'd loitered over a pot of coffee and a stack of wheat cakes in the dining room.

Mabry was frustrated over his inability to get his hands around the Colorado robbery and the soldiers' deaths. Was Garber the culprit or not? He even went so far as to wonder if Fanny Burch was involved somehow. After all, the gold coins did show up in her deposits, and she was quick to deny any knowledge of them. Was it possible she had seen something in the saloon and was hiding it from him? And there was the gold coin that had been found on Smoky Joe to consider as well. He'd been another of those Long Horn loafers.

It could be he had simply read the clues wrong and had showed up at the wrong place. Could it be Captain Rainey's note had led all of them down the wrong trail? *Carrsville. Landing.* Now to hear this business about Dave Harker giving away his family ranch just added to his bewilderment.

Mabry reached the Bar-N around midmorning. Sarge and the boys had dispersed to their jobs long before he arrived. He saw Jeff's horse saddled and tied at the hitching post ready to ride. He also saw a beautiful, wide-chested, red-tinted stallion tied to the post. He had seen two or three Thoroughbreds dur-

177

ing his travels and judged this horse to be of that breed. Captain Peterson sat in one of the rocking chairs talking to a man Mabry hadn't seen before. They had their heads together looking at a book.

"Frank," Captain Peterson said. "Come on up and join us."

Mabry tied off Moses and climbed the steps.

"Frank Mabry, meet Hugh Fowler, a neighbor of mine."

Mabry and Fowler shook hands. "Pleasure to meet you," Mabry said. "That's a beautiful horse you have. A Thoroughbred, I believe?"

Fowler was dressed in the manner of a gentleman rancher: black coat, dark trousers, white shirt, and a string tie. He toyed with a short-stemmed pipe as he talked with Peterson. Mabry judged him to be in his mid-sixties.

"Yes, it's a Kentucky Thoroughbred," Fowler said. "I brought him with me from the east. Zeus is my pride and joy."

"Hugh was showing me a book a friend of his wrote," Peterson said. "It's called *Ben-Hur*. Hugh tells me it's quite a tale."

"The author, Lew Wallace, and I served together briefly during the war," Fowler said. He handed the book to Mabry. "General Wallace even wrote a nice personal inscription inside."

Mabry wasn't much of one to read books—especially thick books like the one he was holding. He stuck with newspapers mostly. But he thought it would be mannerly to seem interested in Fowler's book. He opened it, read the inscription, and then thumbed idly through the pages.

"I might give it a try one of these days," Mabry said, returning the book to Fowler.

"Hugh has a ranch to the east of Carrsville," Peterson said.

"It's a small ranch. Nothing at all like Samuel's ranch. I bought the Whipsaw when I retired, more or less as a way to keep busy. My wife died three years ago back in Maryland and I was at loose ends. When a friend told me about this ranch, I traveled out here. When I saw it, I knew it was exactly what I needed. I don't have it in my blood to be a big rancher like Samuel. I just dabble at it to keep busy."

Mabry thought he would like a chance to dabble at ranching, too. When he'd finished here, he was going to give it a try back at Adairsville. Maybe. If Reed Bannister would leave him alone for a few days.

"We were talking about the Slant-H earlier. Hugh tells me there's talk going around that Dave Harker is turning his ranch over to Hank Garber."

Avery Landing was on target with his prediction that the news would spread in a hurry. Since everyone seemed to know about it, Mabry didn't feel he was breaking his word to Landing about discussing it.

"I heard that, too," Mabry said. "It seems a mighty strange thing for Harker to do. Just hand a large ranch like that over to his foreman."

"I was over at the Slant-H a couple of days ago." Fowler said. "I talked to Hank Garber at length. You're right, it is a strange thing for Harker to do. I don't know Garber all that well, but he acts like a man who has something to hide. He seems preoccupied with his own thoughts at times. Still, I've learned through experience not to jump to conclusions. All this talk about Garber and the Slant-H might have a logical explanation we can't see from a distance."

"You're right, Hugh," Peterson said. "I need to take a closer look at it before I pass judgment."

Fowler then turned to Mabry and said, "I've also heard that you're in the area looking into a robbery of some kind that took place in Kansas. Are you making any progress?"

"It was a train robbery in Colorado. And no, I'm no closer to the answer than when I arrived. I'll give it a few more days here, then move on and hope to find something farther down the line."

Hugh Fowler stood and said, "If I can be of any help, let me know. Now it's time I moved on and let you gentlemen get on with your work. I'll keep you informed about the cattle prices, Samuel."

Samuel escorted Fowler to his horse and waved him away. "Nice man," he said. "And that's a nice horse he's riding, too. I wouldn't mind having one like it for myself."

"What's this he said about cattle prices?"

"Fowler has a friend in Kansas City who says the price of cattle is on the upswing at the rail heads. If that's true, it would solve a lot of our problems. I could get a small herd together pretty quick and be on the move. I think the crew we have here could manage several hundred head without a problem."

Mabry hoped it was true. He knew the Bar-N could use a little good news. He only wished a little of the stardust would fall his way.

CHAPTER FORTY-NINE

Sarge was working the cattle on the northwest section of the Bar-N range. Ranch hands had long ago named that section of the ranch Hell's Holler. The area was covered with a massive growth of thorny brush that made travel in that section perilous at best. The hands had avoided it like the plague. The cattle that grazed there were difficult to bunch, and meandered through the sparse pasture at will. It was one of the areas on the ranch the hands had pretty much ignored since they'd become short-handed. They supposed the cattle in Hell's Holler could take care of themselves.

Sarge had decided early that morning to ride over in that direction to check it out, since he hadn't been there in several weeks. As he rode among the scattered longhorns, he could see their number was down from what he remembered from an earlier inspection. He thought he knew the problem. He rode around the ravine, among the trees, then out into the grassy areas where the bulk of the cattle had gathered. It was there he saw the tracks. Several riders had been to Hell's Holler not too many days before. And they had taken quite a few head of Bar-N cattle with them. He scouted around and decided it was a small drive—maybe fifty head or so. It was apparent to him the rustlers hadn't wanted to put in all the hard work needed to make a larger gathering.

Sarge gazed in the direction the cattle had been driven. Should he go get Gil, or follow them alone? He looked up at the sun. It was getting on into the afternoon. He decided to follow the tracks as far as he could to see where they led. He rode until he reached a point where the trail split off in three directions. One trail led farther into the tree line. A second trail led to the old Adobe Hole silver mine. The third trail just snaked around the foothills not going anywhere in particular. The rustlers' tracks led Sarge farther toward the tree line.

An hour later, Sarge smelled wood smoke drifting toward him. Someone had a campfire burning deep among the trees. He dismounted and tied off his horse. Ahead was a stand of oak and cottonwood trees. He bent low and crept up to get a closer look. As he got nearer, he began to hear voices in the clearing. He eased forward and saw five men gathered around a small campfire. Three army tents stood a few yards away near the trees. These men had been holed up in the clearing for some time.

Sarge recognized three of the men right off: Ike Porter, Slim Willis, and Seth Lomax. The other two men had their backs to him and he couldn't see their faces. He crept as close as he dared, but close enough to hear bits of their conversation. He dropped down on his stomach and stretched out behind a fallen oak tree.

"I say tonight," Porter said. "We've played pitty-pat with these ranchers long enough. Twenty here, thirty there. Let's hit 'em big, get the rest of that train robbery loot, and leave this country for good."

"Ain't nothing holding me here," Slim said. "Besides, I don't like the idea of that marshal hanging around. It's keeping me out here in the boonies. I'm ready to move on to richer territory."

There was more low talk that Sarge couldn't hear. The unknown man then stood and said, "Tonight. We'll hit that herd on the Bar-N first. That'll get us a couple hundred easy. Then we'll hit the Laidlaw ranch next. That'll be another two, three hundred. We can handle all that and be long gone by daybreak."

Porter threw a stick into the fire and said, "Laidlaw and Peterson ain't got enough men to bother us." He let out a loud laugh and added, "Old man Peterson won't know his cattle are gone for more'n a week. His hands don't ever go out to that part of their range."

"All right. I'll be back before midnight. You'd better get some sleep. We'll have to push the cattle hard all night to get them hid in that box canyon with the rest of the herd by daylight."

Sarge backed away from the fallen tree. He'd heard all he needed to hear.

CHAPTER FIFTY

Mabry sat on the porch talking with Jeff and Sara when Sarge came galloping into the yard. His horse skidded to a stop in front of them and Sarge jumped out of the saddle.

Mabry leaped off the porch and grabbed the horse. "Whoa, Sarge. You're too old to be rodeo-ing like that. Slow down."

"You ain't seen no rodeo yet, Mabry. But it's about to happen." Sarge described to his audience of three what he'd discovered at Hell's Holler, and what he'd heard in the clearing at the grove of trees.

"They're going to hit tonight, you say?"

"That's what I heard. They're planning on hitting the Bar-N first, then the Laidlaw place after that. It sounds like they're planning a big roundup and then skedaddling with the cattle to some box canyon where they have another herd hid away."

Mabry turned to Sara and said, "Sara, would you ride out and round up Gil, Earl, and Rob? You probably know where they can be found. We'll stay here and see what we can do to mess up their plans."

Sara hurried down the steps and took off on Jeff's horse.

"It sounds like my old friends, Ike Porter and Slim, are still around causing us problems. I never believed they'd left the territory."

Sarge took the reins of his horse from Mabry and said, "The way they sounded, I expect they've been hiding out in the backwoods ever since Jeff here ruined their fun. And another thing. I heard one of them say something about getting the rest of that train robbery loot and leaving the country. This bunch might be tied in with your Colorado robbery, too."

Mabry glanced at Jeff and said, "It looks like things are ready to bust wide open around here, Lieutenant Keener. I expect we should help it along any way we can."

"Where's the captain?" Sarge asked. "He needs to be in on this confab."

"He's got a burr under his saddle about Dave Harker giving away his ranch. He's out riding and thinking. He'll be back before long."

They were all there: Peterson, Mabry, Jeff, and the four ranch hands. The whole group sat at the table after the evening meal drinking coffee and munching on Hannah's teacakes. Samuel Peterson sat at the head of the table as usual. Mabry sat on his right.

Sarge told his story once again, answering questions as he went.

Mabry could see a few anxious glances among them. Gil Alvarez was chomping at the bit; ready to go after the rustlers. Sarge kept trying to calm him down. The two old-timers, Earl Pickens and Rob Calhoun, looked ready to ride as well.

"We could charge into their camp," Peterson said. "We might get one or two that way. But if they have lookouts, we might not get any of them." He scanned the table, and his gaze landed on Pickens and Calhoun. "Earl, you and Rob don't have to be a part of this. If you want out that's no problem. The rest of us have been in these kind of skirmishes before."

"We hired on here a lotta years ago, Cap'n. I reckon we'll do what we can to stay on another few years," Pickens said. "We've fit off two-legged varmints before."

"Then we have seven of us here," Peterson said. "Sara has

gone to get Sheriff Tolliver to make sure we do it all legal like. That'll make eight. More, if he brings along any deputies. According to Sarge, we can expect about four or five of the bad guys. If we get in position ahead of them, we can set a trap and let 'em ride straight into it."

"There's really only one way into that narrow hollow from where they're camped," Sarge said. "It's kinda like a funnel. There are so many trees and scrub bushes growing there, that even the cattle had to make their own trails in and out."

"That helps," Mabry said. "But it sounds like Porter and his gang might have a hard time getting the cattle bunched and driven out."

"From what I heard, they don't think they need to hurry."

Captain Peterson stood and said, "It's about as dark as it's going to get. Let's move out that way and get ourselves in position well ahead of them. If they choose to come early, we'll be waiting. Get your gear ready, men. We'll head out as soon as Sheriff Tolliver gets here. We'll put an end to all this rustling here and now."

"One more thing," Mabry said. "If it comes down to gunplay out there, I want one of them alive. I need some answers about that train robbery."

When the others had left the room, Mabry asked Peterson, "What conclusions did you draw about the Slant-H?"

"Not a blasted thing. This outfit Sarge found has me worried though. I've heard that Slim Willis and Ike Porter have worked for Garber a few times in the past. They've got too many ties with the Slant-H for my money. I still can't believe Dave Harker would go along with anything like this."

Mabry cocked his head at the captain. "*If* Harker knows anything about it," he said. "Don't forget Dave Harker has been housebound for several months. He might not know everything that's going on at the ranch."

Peterson nodded. "Yeah. That bothers me, too."

CHAPTER FIFTY-ONE

When the Bar-N men arrived at Hell's Holler, Mabry listened as Samuel Peterson took charge of placing them in position. He and Sheriff Tolliver were more than pleased to turn the job over to the captain, who had regained some of his old feistiness. Sarge had scouted ahead of them and had brought back word he hadn't seen any sign of rustlers in the hollow.

At the hollow, Mabry, Calhoun, and a deputy named Kelleher were positioned on the east side of the trail the rustlers were likely to take to get to the cattle. Peterson placed Sheriff Tolliver and Gil Alvarez on the west side, at an angle away from Mabry's and Calhoun's line of fire. Straight in front, he placed Earl Pickens and Jeff. Peterson and Sarge were going to be the corks in the bottle if any of the rustlers tried to escape back down the trail—which was likely. They would remain hunkered down and away from the various lines of fire as well.

Mabry glanced up at the sky. The clouds were thick and moving so that the half-moon's glow came and went. That, along with the thick canopy of branches and leaves, gave them limited vision of no more than a couple hundred yards. Mabry looked over at Rob Calhoun, who was stretched out on the ground with his hat pulled low over his eyes. Mabry grinned. The old man was catching a few winks.

It was well after midnight when Mabry nudged Calhoun in the ribs with the toe of his boot. "I hear horses, Rob. Better get ready."

Calhoun rolled over and crawled up beside Mabry and Kelle-her. "Kinda like Chickamauga. Sleep a little, fight a little." Calhoun cut off a hunk of tobacco and poked it into his jaw. "I ain't fired this old Springfield in anger in nigh on to fifteen years. Hope I ain't forgot how."

Mabry pointed down the trail. He could see movement. "Here they come. Remember, Peterson is going to give them a chance to throw down their guns and give up without a fight."

"Don't expect that'll work," Calhoun said.

"Me neither, so be ready."

As the riders got closer, Mabry began to recognize a few of them. Ike Porter was in front, followed by Slim. He counted three other men behind Slim; five of them in all. Mabry laid his Winchester across a log and waited as the outlaws rode past in single file not twenty yards away.

Then he heard Captain Peterson shout, "Throw down your guns, Porter. Now. You're surrounded."

Everything after that shout was a blur. As expected, instead of throwing down their guns, the rustlers began firing wildly. That was followed by a return volley from the surrounding trees. Mabry stood up and fired at a man who had wheeled his horse around and ran straight at him. The man tumbled off the horse. He could hear bullets whistling all around.

"Pretty fair shooting, Marshal," Calhoun said. "I think I mighta got one of them buzzards, too."

The shooting stopped within minutes. Mabry could see that one of the riders had thrown down his guns and was holding up his hands. Three more men were lying on the ground. A fifth rider had disappeared into the trees.

Sheriff Tolliver ran in from the trees and held his gun on the lone mounted rustler. "Hands high, Ike," Tolliver shouted. Tolliver was quickly joined by the others.

"Anybody hurt?" Peterson asked, looking around at the

Bar-N hands.

No one answered, but Mabry could account for all of them. He walked over to one of the men who was squirming on the ground and moaning. It was Slim. He had a taken a bullet in his abdomen. Mabry knew it was a bad wound.

"Who's behind all this, Slim?" Mabry asked. "You might as well talk. No sense leaving here with this hanging over your head. What do you say? Were you involved in the Colorado train robbery?"

"Yeah . . . me and . . . the . . . others."

"Give me names, Slim."

Mabry watched as Slim's eyes blinked, then closed. He was still breathing, barely hanging on. Mabry felt a hand on his shoulder. He looked up and saw it was Sheriff Tolliver.

"Tell him what he wants to know, Slim," Tolliver said.

Slim grabbed Mabry's arm and stared at him with blank, watery eyes. "Ju . . . Ju . . . Junior." Then he collapsed back to the ground. Slim Willis had spoken his last word.

"Did he say Junior?" Tolliver asked.

"That's what he said."

Tolliver shook his head. "I've lived here all my life, and I never heard anyone called that around here."

Mabry stood and looked down at the man who had wanted Ike Porter to kill him a few days earlier. Now he was dead. Porter sat on a horse just a few feet away. Mabry hurried over to Porter and asked, "Who's behind all this, Porter? Tell me, or I'm going to do to you what you did to me. Then I'm going to let Sarge take a turn at you. Believe me, you don't want that man punching you. Now give me names. We'll start with Junior. Who's Junior?"

"I'll tell if you'll let me go."

Mabry reached up and was about to jerk Porter off his horse when a shot rang out from the trees. Porter clutched at his chest and tumbled to the ground. Mabry dropped on his stomach and rolled away from Porter's body. No more shots came from the trees. From his left, Sarge, Gil, and the others let loose with a volley of lead in the direction of the gunshot that shook the ground. Mabry then heard the sound of hooves. To his surprise, he saw Lieutenant Keener take off into the trees after the escaping rustler.

After the few minutes of excitement was over. Mabry looked down at Ike Porter. He was dead when he hit the ground. His hope of getting information about the train robbery now rested with the rustler who got away.

Sheriff Tolliver and his deputy hauled all the dead bodies to the center of the hollow. They lined them up on their backs. "It looks like Slim, Ike, Lomax, and Tosh Willard are all dead," Tolliver said. "I always suspected them of being involved with the rustling. I just never could prove it was them. I guess I won't have to now. I'd say we've had a right good night, all in all."

Mabry had to agree with Tolliver with one exception. He still didn't know who was behind all this. And he wondered who had managed to escape their trap.

"Did you get a look at the other one, Sheriff?" Mabry asked. "The one who got away?"

"No. I was too busy shooting. I doubt he'll be hanging around now with all his cohorts stretched out in the dust. He'd be smart to keep riding."

That's exactly what Mabry was afraid he'd do.

Chapter Fifty-Two

The Bar-N men spent another hour helping Sheriff Tolliver and Deputy Kelleher wrap up the details. Kelleher, along with Sarge and Gil, had tied the dead men across their horses for the trip back to Carrsville.

"I believe we made a big dent in the rustling around here tonight, Samuel," Tolliver said. "If not, then we've certainly sent them a warning that we're not standing pat any longer."

"These four won't be bothering us, that's for sure."

"Captain, I'll put Sarge and Gil up overnight at the hotel if you'll let them help me and Kelleher get the bodies back to Carrsville."

Sarge heard the comment and rushed over to join the two men. He stood there kicking at the dirt, waiting for Peterson to answer.

Peterson grinned. "Of course, Sheriff." He turned to Sarge and said, "Why don't you and Gil take the day off tomorrow? It's been a long time since you've been able to cut loose. You've earned it. I think we can spare you for a while."

"Why, that's real accommodating of you, Cap'n. Don't you think so, Gil?"

"Plumb accommodating," Gil said. "We'll see you in a day—or two."

Mabry was exhausted and drained of all energy. It was always that way for him after a confrontation with outlaws. He felt a little renewed when he saw Jeff return from his pursuit of the lone escapee. He wouldn't admit it to anyone, but he'd taken quite a big liking for the kid.

"I lost him in the dark," Jeff said. "The trail split into several directions near the foothills, and it was too dark to see which one he had taken." Jeff took off his hat and brushed a hand back over his hair. "It might've been my imagination, but I thought I saw a light flickering in the distance through the trees."

Peterson shrugged. "Mighta been the moon's reflection. All that's down that way is what's left of an old mining operation."

"I'm going back to Carrsville with the sheriff, too," Mabry said. "I'll be back at the ranch tomorrow or the next day. I'm going to try to find out the name of that fifth rustler. Someone around town knows who he is. I've just got to find that person."

"Don't you go off and do something foolish while I'm not watching," Jeff said.

Mabry grinned and rode away with Sheriff Tolliver.

Chapter Fifty-Three

Coy Dickson had found a line shack on the back side of the Slant-H ranch after riding hard for several miles. Dickson scrambled into the shack and fell across a braided rope cot, tired and tense after the gunfight and the long ride. When he'd heard the shout coming from the trees, he had known they were in trouble. The narrow trail and the thick growth of trees spelled danger all around. He hadn't hesitated. He had jerked the reins on his horse and made a mad dash toward the thickest brush he could find. Behind him, he heard the explosion of gunfire. That was Slim and Lomax for you. They always thought they could shoot their way out of anything.

Concealed in the thick brush, he had watched as Slim went down early on, then Lomax and Willard. As for Ike Porter, he would've talked his head off in a matter of minutes. Dickson realized he was taking a chance by shooting that weasel, but his concern was solely for himself now. He pulled the trigger and took off as fast as the terrain would let him.

It was tough going through the thick brush at night: needle-like thorns, low limbs, and the tomb-like darkness made his travel near impossible. He felt the brush tearing at his clothes. He kept his head ducked low to keep from getting an eye punched out by a sharp limb. Then he heard someone behind him. Someone was following him. Or could it be more than one?

Dickson trudged on and soon became convinced he'd lost his

pursuer. He dabbed his bandanna at the scratches on his face and slowed his horse to a walk. It was just after daybreak when he ran across the line shack. He sat up on the cot and lightly touched his bleeding left shoulder. His shirt had been shredded by the thorns, so he ripped it off to examine the wound. It was a deep cut caused by a thorn bush. He tore a piece off the shirt and held it against the wound while he searched through the shack. In a box under the cot, Dickson found a ragged shirt that had been discarded long ago by a cowboy. It was stiff and stank to the high heavens, but it would have to do. The only other thing he found of use was a whiskey bottle with maybe half an inch left in it. He'd heard talk that some of those thorn bushes were poisonous, so the whiskey was a lucky find.

Dickson took the piece of shirt from his shoulder, doused it with the remaining whiskey, and pressed it to his wound. He clenched his teeth as the alcohol sent a burning sensation up and down his arm. He sat down on the cot again and tried to think out his next move. If he was smart, he would climb into his saddle and ride toward the Indian Nation. That would be the safe play.

But Junior held the train robbery money—and Dickson wanted it. He wasn't about to leave over four hundred thousand dollars in the hands of that double-dealer. Dickson made up his mind then and there. He would go after Junior, get the rest of the money, and then ride hard for the Indian Nation. There he would lie low and enjoy the fruits of their labor. With that decision made, Dickson fell back on the cot and closed his eyes.

Tomorrow, he thought, as sleep enveloped him.

CHAPTER FIFTY-FOUR

Jeff had been doing some serious thinking of his own. So far in their pursuit of the killers, he'd been relegated to a supporting role. He had understood from the beginning that would be the case. Maybe it was due to his age and his relative inexperience. Still, he was an officer in the U.S. Army; an officer who had been given an important assignment right from the highest offices in the land. With Mabry going to be in Carrsville, he saw that the ground had been cleared for him to assert himself without having the marshal looking over his shoulder.

The morning after the rustlers had been dealt with, Jeff searched out Sara and found her talking to her mother in the kitchen. Sarge and Gil were in Carrsville living it up for the first time in a long while, so it was quiet around the ranch.

Jeff took Sara by the arm and said, "Let's go out on the porch and talk for a bit."

The morning was cloudless and bright. Jeff found himself getting used to the sounds of a Texas ranch: the bawling cows, horses stomping on the hard-packed ground, and even the rowdy laughter and shouting coming from the bunkhouse. As surprised as he was at the thought, he had begun to enjoy the sounds. He guessed western life was growing on him. As was the freckle-faced Sara.

Jeff pulled Sara over into the shadows of the porch and put his hands around her oval-shaped face. He looked into her eyes and saw that she did not flinch from his familiarity. He leaned in and kissed her, then backed away. "I've been wanting to do that from the first time I saw you on the hotel veranda."

"I guess it was the next morning in the lobby for me," she said. She stepped in closer and they kissed again. After a few minutes, she said, "In this particular area I've got to admit I'm the greenhorn. I can shoot and ride with the best of them, and I've got a reputation for creating havoc just about everywhere I go. But, Lieutenant Keener, this is something I've not had any experience with."

"We'll go about it slow," he said. "When this is all over, we'll have time to think about it more seriously."

He took her hand and led her over to the rocking chairs. He pulled them close together so they could still hold hands. Jeff said, "You know the layout of the Bar-N ranch pretty well, don't you? The land and terrain all around the ranch?"

"Sure. I've ridden all over this place. There's not a place I haven't been. Why're you asking?"

Jeff told her about him chasing the escaped rustler, and of seeing a light through the branches. He told her that her father had dismissed it as his imagination. Jeff said he wasn't so sure.

"I'd like to go over there and look around a little. There's something about that whole setup that seems to be off. The rustlers came from that direction, and I still believe I saw a flickering light. Like a lantern might give off. I'd like to know for sure."

"You can't just ride over there and start poking around if you think someone might be living there. That would be too dangerous."

He could hear the skepticism in her voice. And she might have a valid point. Still, this was something he felt a need to do. "I have to do this, Sara. I'll be back before dark. I promise."

Sara shook her head. "No, Jeff. You can't go gallivanting out there all alone. You don't know the country. If you're determined to go, I'm going with you."

"I think one person acting alone would have a better chance than two. There would be less chance of being spotted. It shouldn't be too hard to find the trail in broad daylight."

She leaned over and kissed him, then let go of his hand. She stepped over to the edge of the porch and said, "That's a brave thing you're wanting to do, Jeff. But it's a bit on the foolish side, too. If you're right, you should wait for Mabry, or Sarge, or Gil."

He went over and stood beside her. "I'll be careful, freckle-face, I promise."

CHAPTER FIFTY-FIVE

It was midmorning by the time Coy Dickson reached the ranch. When he had finished his business with Junior, he was never going to be seen around Carrsville again. He rode up to the rear of the house and dismounted. While his left shoulder still stung, it had not hampered his movement in any way. Dickson entered the cabin, shouted, and found it empty. Junior was most likely out with his hands.

He scrounged around the cabin and found a shirt that fit—and smelled better than the one he'd found last night. While he was there, he opened all the closets, armoires, desk drawers, and likely hiding places for anything valuable. Dickson found a few dollars, but not much else useful to him.

He had been waiting over an hour when Junior returned.

"Dickson," Junior said. "This is the second time you've come here against my express wishes."

Dickson took a few steps toward Junior and said, "Me and you gotta take care of our business now. We can't wait any longer." He told Junior about the gunfight with the sheriff and the Bar-N hands. "Porter, Lomax, Slim, and Tosh Willard were all killed in the shootout. I barely got away. I've got to leave the area pronto. The sheriff and that marshal will be scouring the country looking for me."

Junior stood with a look of concern on his face. "They don't know about your connection with me, do they?"

Dickson shook his head. "Nope. I ain't told nobody our little secret. But time's up. No more waiting. I want that money now."

"We'll have to wait until dark. We can't take a chance of being seen out in the open. There's too many people around here."

"I don't give a damn about being seen anymore. We're going after the money now. After that, I'm leaving this country behind me for good. If you're smart, you'll do the same."

"If I leave now, they'll know I was involved. I can't go. Besides, with you gone, nobody will be able to connect me to the robbery. I say we wait until it gets dark and not take any chances."

Dickson pulled his gun. "We're going now. So let's get moving. I don't have time to wait around any longer."

CHAPTER FIFTY-SIX

The trail the Bar-N men had used the previous night was plainly visible to Jeff. He had no trouble following it back to Hell's Holler. Once there, he had no problem recognizing the spot where he had taken off after the escaping rustler. The terrain looked much different in daylight, but he soon found the tracks left by his horse. The tracks led him back to where the trails had split. Off to the west, he could see the foothills. It was to the left of that direction where he had seen the glow of light through the trees.

He rode for several minutes until he came to the rise in the trail. Being cautious, he dismounted and crept up to the top of the rise. He could see a stone building and what remained of the mining operation Captain Peterson had mentioned. It reminded him of an old junkyard he'd once seen back in Boston: rusted equipment piled on top of other rusted equipment, broken wheels, and piles of split support timbers. He scanned the area and didn't see any sign of life.

Jeff had earlier noticed a dry creek bed that ran parallel to the trail. He returned to his horse and tied it off to a lightning-struck oak tree. He could go from there on foot to the mine without being seen should there be someone nearby.

The weeds around the mine were knee-high, and there were enough trees scattered between him and the stone building for cover. He darted from one tree to another until he was within a few yards of the stone building. He stopped and listened. Nothing but a few crows cawing off in the distance. He remained still for a full ten minutes, listening and watching. Once he was satisfied he was alone, he crept up to the door of the building. Still quiet. No sounds or movement around the building. He opened the door and peered inside. As his eyes became accustomed to the dim light, he moved forward. It had taken only a few steps into the building for him to realize the building was now occupied. A full bottle of whiskey sat on the table, along with scraps of bread on a tin plate. A deck of cards laid out as a solitaire game was spread on the table. Over in the corner was a cot with blankets and a pillow. And a coal oil lantern sat near the building's side window. Someone had set up housekeeping in the building.

As he looked around, he heard a sound behind the building. Someone was singing. He listened and recognized the song. It was an old Irish song: "The Gown of Green." He'd heard his mother sing it often back in Boston.

There was no place in the one-room building for him to hide. Jeff stood still and listened as the singing continued. The singer came closer and closer. He eased over to the grimy window and peeked through. He saw a man standing in front of the mine entrance still singing softly. Jeff saw that he was carrying a rifle in his left hand.

Escape through the rear door was out of the question. He looked around. Maybe escape through the front door was possible if the singer would stay away for a few more minutes. Jeff tiptoed to the door and pulled it open slowly. He was relieved the metal hinges didn't creak. He stepped out into the daylight and beat a retreat back toward his horse.

Jeff had his foot in the stirrup when the man stepped out from behind the lightning-struck tree and stuck a gun in his ribs.

"What're you doing snooping around here?"

While Jeff was trying to think of a logical explanation, the man hit him over the head with the butt of his rifle.

CHAPTER FIFTY-SEVEN

Mabry was joined in the Carrsville Hotel dining room by Sarge and Gil. By the time the sheriff's group had reached Carrsville with the rustlers' bodies, it was near daylight. The three ex-Rangers had slept past noon the following morning and awakened weary from the long night at Hell's Holler. The three of them had little to say to each other. They just attacked their ham and eggs with vigor.

Mabry finished his meal first and leaned back in his chair with a cup of coffee. "You two scoundrels going to raise a ruckus tonight?"

Sarge shook his head. "Not if I feel like this. Besides, it's been so long since I've seen a ruckus, I probably wouldn't recognize it if I was in one."

"He'll feel better once he gets his eyes open," Gil said. "Me? I'm not passing up this opportunity."

Mabry threw some coins on the table. "The meals on the army, boys. I've gotta get going."

The telegraph office was Mabry's first stop. The Western Union operator was whistling while he swept the floor when Mabry entered. He propped the broom in the corner of the office and smiled at his customer.

"Morning," Mabry said. "I need to send a message to Dallas." He spent the next ten minutes gathering his thoughts before putting them on paper. After he was satisfied he knew what questions he needed answered, he wrote the message.

"I expect a reply to this message," Mabry said. "I'll check back tomorrow or the next day."

The Long Horn Saloon still had its loafers hanging around the steps of the boardwalk. And they still kept their eyes on the marshal as he got nearer. When he reached the front of the saloon, Mabry saw the grizzled old man holding court in the same place as before. Mabry stopped in front of him and asked, "Remember me, old-timer?"

"Hee, hee," the old man said with a laugh. "Course I 'member you. You're the man who put the whupping on old Rad Bascom." He pointed at the street. "Right there. In front of God and everybody."

"Yep. That was me."

"And I 'spect it was you who ran him outta town, too."

"Yep. That was me."

"Ain't no big loss. Fact is, some would likely buy you a drink for drivin' him outta town."

Mabry patted the old man on the shoulder and brushed past him into the saloon. There were six to eight men standing around. Some drinking, some playing poker, most loafing. Fanny Burch wasn't in sight. Mabry stepped up to the bar, ordered a beer, and turned to survey the room. He saw a few of the men glance at him, then turn away. Others stared at the sawdusty floor when Mabry looked in their direction. Mabry was sure the word of the scrap out at the Bar-N had already made the rounds. The rough crowd was keeping out of sight for a while. If he asked, he doubted he'd find anyone who'd own up to knowing Ike Porter.

Mabry was chatting with Louie the bartender when he spotted Fanny Burch ambling toward him from the stairway. She had a smile on her face.

"Still stirring up trouble, aren't you, Mabry?" She joined him at the bar and leaned back against it. "Some men thrive when they're in the midst of discord and turmoil. I've come to the conclusion that you're the chief of that tribe."

"Like I told you, Fanny. That's my lot in life."

She laughed. "So, tell me. Have you made any progress in locating the stolen money?"

"Not yet."

"You know you're about to ruin my business, don't you?"

"How's that?"

"I wasn't born yesterday, as you can tell. I have a sneaky feeling you're planning to clean out all the riffraff within fifty miles of this place. Ike Porter and the gang that ran with him had more spending money than any bunch of cowpokes I've ever run across. You're about to change everything around here, aren't you?"

Mabry nodded. "I'm going after every last one of those men who are behind the robbery, the killings, and the rustling. I have every confidence you'll survive just fine, Fanny. Avery Landing over at the bank says you're clever and resourceful. You'll make out all right. In fact, I'd lay down odds that you'll do even better with that gang of cutthroats like Porter and Slim out of your hair. But I would suggest that you clean up this place. Maybe even fumigate it. You might be surprised at how well you would do with some regular upstanding customers."

"That's a good suggestion. Now let me tell you something. After you ruin my business, you're still welcome to come back anytime you please. Remember that open invitation?"

He smiled and said, "How could I forget?"

She gave him a playful little slap on the cheek and said, "And I mean anytime."

"I'll be back. It's the blue door, right?" Mabry then nodded toward her office. "Right now I need to ask you something. In private." He closed the office door behind them and asked,

"Who did Porter and Slim answer to? They weren't smart enough to get away with all this rustling business by themselves. Who called the shots for them?"

"I honestly don't know, Mabry. Louie might know. He doesn't miss much that goes on around here."

Fanny opened the door, got the bartender's attention, and called him over. "Mabry wants some information," she said. "Help him out if you can."

"Fanny said you hear a little of everything that goes on around here, Louie. I want to know who Ike and Slim rode with. I don't think they had the brains to create all this turmoil by themselves."

Louie took the toothpick out of his mouth and said, "There's a man who comes in here every now and agin who likes to gamble. A small man; he don't weigh much more than a good sized kid." Louie ran a finger down his cheek. "He's got a scar that runs from here to here. He don't show up every night, but when he does show, he stays until we lock the doors. Ike, Slim, and a couple others defer to him like he's the boss. I once heard Slim call him Coy. That's all I can tell you."

Coy. Coy Dickson.

Mabry had known of the outlaw for several years. As far as he could recall, he'd never had any personal dealings with Dickson. From what he'd heard about the man, Dickson was smart, dangerous, and totally ruthless. The Colorado train robbery would have fit him perfectly.

Mabry handed the bartender a fistful of bills. "Let the house drink until you use it all up, Louie. It's on the government. And thanks for the information."

On his way out of the saloon, he met Sheriff Tolliver on the boardwalk.

"It's been a quiet day so far," Tolliver said. "What're you going to do to mess it up for me?"

"It's people like me who keep getting you re-elected, Sheriff," Mabry said. He took hold of the sheriff's arm and pulled him out into the street. "I've got to send another telegram, Sheriff, then me and you are going to look at some wanted posters. I might be able to create some more votes for you come election time."

At the sheriff's office, Tolliver emptied his desk drawers of all the wanted posters he could find. He stacked them in front of Mabry, who sat at the sheriff's desk. Most of the posters were yellowed, brittle, and out of date.

"This is one way to get my office cleaned up," Tolliver said.

Mabry had thumbed through some fifty or more posters when he found the one he'd been looking for. He smiled and handed it to Sheriff Tolliver. "You ever see this man around Carrsville?"

Tolliver pulled out a pair of wire-rimmed glasses and gazed at the artist's rendering of Coy Dickson. He held it close, then back at arm's length. He shrugged. "It's hard to tell from this picture." He handed the poster back to Mabry. "Coy Dickson, huh? I've heard talk of him. He's supposed to be a bad *hombre*."

Mabry was certain Dickson was tied in with the Colorado robbery and the related killings. Now all he had to do was find him.

CHAPTER FIFTY-EIGHT

At the morning meal, Sara felt her heart beating so hard she thought it was going to burst. Jeff had not returned during the night like he had promised her. She had stayed awake all night listening for him. What was she to do?

It's my fault. I should have stopped him.

Sara broke into tears as she helped her mother clear away the dishes. She hurried out to the back porch and sat on the steps. There had been a moment of hope at sunrise when she'd heard horses' hooves outside her window. She rushed to take a look. Her heart sank as she saw Earl Pickens headed out on the range. She wiped at her eyes, thinking of Jeff out there all alone, hurt—or worse.

She wiped at her eyes again and took a deep breath. She didn't want her mother to see her crying. How could she explain it? She had to do something, but what? She stared at her hands as all kinds of thoughts swirled through her mind. Jeff thrown from a horse. Jeff shot. She reached down and picked up a small stone. Sara rolled the stone around in her fingers, then slung it across the yard. She could sit around and mope all day, or she could do something.

She ran to the barn and saddled her horse. "Tell Dad I'm going out for a ride," she said to Rob Calhoun. "I'll be back a little later."

"Your dad has gone into town, Sara. You be careful now, you hear?"

It was late morning when Sara left the Bar-N. She knew where Jeff had intended to go, so she would ride hard in that direction. She spurred her horse and headed toward Hell's Holler. She felt anxious about going there, knowing Jeff might be out there somewhere injured.

When she reached Hell's Holler, she was both disappointed and relieved that she didn't find him there. He had told her about chasing the one rustler who had escaped, so she searched around until she found the hoofprints where the trail split off in different directions. She knew Jeff's tracks would lead to the old Adobe Hole Mine.

Sara slowed her horse to a walk as she approached the abandoned mine. When she neared the mine, she moved off the trail into the bushes. From a ridge behind the stone building, she looked down at the mine yard. She saw a horse tied to a broken-down wagon. It was the horse Jeff had ridden. She had found him.

But why was his horse there? She continued to scan the area below her. Sara backed off the ridge and returned to her horse, where she stopped to think about what to do next. She was convinced in her own mind that Jeff was not at the building of his own accord. Sara was sure Jeff would have returned to the ranch if at all possible.

She could either go get her dad and the men at the ranch, or she could take it upon herself to help him.

As she thought about these things, the decision was made for her.

"Hey, little gal. Have you lost your way?"

Sara jerked her head around and saw a man standing there. He was a thin, older man with one arm, who carried a rifle in his left hand. She had never seen him before.

"Come on, little gal. Let's take a walk. You can see better down there."

★ ★ ★ ★ ★

Jeff Keener was stretched out on a blanket in a low-roofed shaft in the silver mine. Padlocked iron bars separated him from the main shaft, and the outside world. A one-armed man had shoved him into the shaft after he had been questioned for a few minutes. He was pleased that he had resisted telling the man anything of importance. Of course, everyone in Carrsville knew of his and Mabry's reasons for being there. There was little else for anyone to learn.

Other than how stupid he'd been to try such a dumb stunt. He should've listened to Sara.

All he saw in the dark recesses of the mine was a lantern, a bucket of water, and the stiff, stinking horse blanket. He lay there and studied the situation. He knew he wasn't a genius, but neither was he an idiot. There had to be a way out. He just had to find it.

Jeff crawled around in the dingy shaft, poking and digging at every spot that looked promising. At the back of the shaft he found a tall wooden door that looked as though it hadn't been opened in years. *Danger High Explosives* was painted on the door in crude letters. The door's hinges and latches were covered in rust. As he drew closer to the door, he could see a bluish liquid dripping from the bottom of the top hinge. He touched the liquid, then rubbed it between his thumb and index finger. Oil.

Someone had recently oiled the hinges to the door. There was a chain that looped through the door, but no lock. He pulled the chain free and tried to open the door. The door was wedged closed by its tight fit into the door jamb. He had to get it open. On the other side there might be a door to the outside he could use to escape. Jeff worked up a sweat as he made a futile effort to get his fingers into a crack.

After an hour, he sat down to study it some more.

Then Jeff caught sight of the lantern's metal handle. It might do the job. He pried the metal hanger off the lantern and straightened it enough to jam into the widest crack he could find. He hoped it was stiff enough for him to pry the door open far enough to get a finger grip. He grunted and pried with all his strength. The lantern handle began to bend under the pressure, then he heard a snap as the door popped open a couple of inches. It opened just enough for him to get a finger grip on the inside of the door. He pulled and tugged at the door for several minutes. Finally, he was able to get a grip with both hands, and gave it a hard jerk. The door opened. Jeff offered a silent prayer that another door to the outside would be there. To his dismay, there was no door.

But there was something else there. Something much more surprising.

Chapter Fifty-Nine

Jeff was pacing the small shaft when he heard the iron bars to the mine entrance open. He turned in time to see the one-armed man push someone into the shed, then slam the gate shut again. He watched in the dim light as the person got up on her hands and knees.

Her hands and knees.

He hurried over to the woman. He bent down and said, "Are you hurt?"

Sara lifted her head and said, "Hello, Jeff. I've come to rescue you."

"Sara! What in blazes are you doing here?"

"What did I just say? I said I came to rescue you."

"And you're doing a fine job of it, too," he said, as he backed away from her. "Are you out of your mind?"

"Funny," she said. "At least I'm halfway there now. I found you."

"The other half might be a bit more difficult—the getting out of here half."

Jeff told her everything that had happened to him since he'd been caught. When he had finished his tale, he pulled her over to a dark corner of the mine and pointed. "See that? I think we might have stumbled on something important."

Sara moved past him. "What is it?"

Jeff pulled the tall door open. "If I'm not mistaken, we've

found the money that was stolen during the Colorado train robbery."

Sara moved past him to get a better view of the metal boxes stacked three high in three columns. Alongside were two canvas bags. All had *U.S. Government* stenciled in black on them.

"We've got to get out of here and tell Mabry," she said.

"I've tried everything I know to do, and I still can't find a way out of this dungeon."

She started banging away at the iron bars that had them imprisoned. "We have to find a way to get out of here. This is too great a discovery."

Jeff shook his head. "You're wasting your energy. I poked and punched every inch of this place. It's solid rock."

"Well, dang it," she said.

CHAPTER SIXTY

The abandoned mine was a great hiding place, Dickson thought, as they pulled up to the stone building. Junior had thought it out well. After he dismounted, a one-armed man came out of the building holding a rifle.

"Dickson," Winters said, his left hand on the rifle's trigger.

"Ease up, Harlan," Dickson said. "I'm after money, not a fight." Dickson looked around and added, "I've ridden all around this place for weeks and never dreamed this was your hiding place."

"Didn't want you to know," Winters said.

Dickson turned away without commenting. "Let's get on with it," he said to Junior. "I've gotta get out of this territory."

Winters sidled up to Junior, pointed to the mine, and said, "I've done cotched me a couple of meddlers."

"Meddlers? What does he mean, Junior?" Dickson asked.

"I don't know. Explain yourself, Harlan."

Harlan then explained how he'd caught a young man sneaking around the mine. Then how he'd later caught a young girl doing the same.

"What did you do with them?"

"I threw 'em in the mine and locked the gate. They're still in there if you want to check 'em out. They don't appear to be any threat."

"I want to talk to them," Dickson said.

"You go ahead," Junior said. "I don't want to be seen here by anyone."

Winters handed the padlock key to Dickson, who took the key and headed for the mine. He unlocked the gate and swung it open. A young man and woman sat huddled together on a blanket in the corner. The girl appeared to be sleeping. The man sat up as Dickson approached them.

"Who are you?" Dickson asked.

The young man hesitated, obviously trying to decide how to answer the simple question.

Dickson kicked him in the side and repeated the question. "I said, who are you?"

"Jeff Keener," the young man said. He nodded at the girl who had awakened. "Her name is Sara Peterson."

"Peterson, huh? She kin to that old Ranger over at the Bar-N?"

"I'm his daughter," Sara said, wiping at her eyes. "And who're you? And why have you locked us up in this stinking place? Dad's going to be awful mad when he finds out about this."

Dickson nodded at Jeff and said, "It was you who followed me after that shootout, wasn't it? That's how you ended up in this fix." Dickson stared at the two young people for a moment, then left the mine, locking the gate behind him. He returned to where Winters and Junior were talking.

"Their names are Jeff Keener and Sara Peterson," Dickson said. "She's the daughter of that Ranger that owns the Bar-N. I don't know anything about Keener."

"I know about Jeff Keener," Junior said. "He's an army officer, the son of a prominent judge in Boston. We can't harm either of them or we'll be in deep trouble."

"They know too much," Dickson said. He checked the loads in his pistol and turned back toward the mine entrance. "We don't need any witnesses."

CHAPTER SIXTY-ONE

It was early afternoon when Captain Peterson finally ran Mabry down in the sheriff's office. Peterson had been weighing the pros and cons of confronting Dave Harker and Hank Garber and had come to a decision. And as a precaution, he wanted Mabry to know where he was going.

"I've thought it over, Frank," Peterson said. "I've put off doing this too long. I'm going over to see Dave Harker and find out what's going on once and for all. If Garber is there, all the better. I'm going to get some answers one way or the other. I've had enough of this foolishness."

Mabry said, "I'll ride along, too."

"No. I think this is something I need to do myself. I just wanted you to know where I was going."

Mabry told Peterson he would wait for him at the sheriff's office and they could return to the Bar-N together.

Samuel Peterson didn't stop to ring the bell at the Slant-H entrance. He had never asked permission to visit Dave in the old days, and he wasn't going to start today. He spurred his mount and rode down the entrance. Surprisingly, he reached the ranch house before he was noticed. A young man carrying a shovel and smelling of horse manure stopped him in front of the house.

"Hey, mister. Didn't you see the sign back yonder? You're supposed to ring the bell before coming in."

"Can't read, son," Peterson said. "Is your boss around?"

"Which boss?"

"Doesn't make any difference which one. Why don't you go look one of 'em up and tell him Samuel Peterson would like a word with him."

The young cowpoke backed away, then hurried to the barn. In a minute, Sam saw Hank Garber head toward him. Garber had his hat in his hand and was wiping his forehead with a red bandanna. He supposed he'd interrupted Garber while he was hard at some job. That was like Dave used to be. Don't ask the ranch hands to do something you won't do yourself.

Garber stopped at Peterson's horse. "Mr. Peterson," Garber said. "What can I do for you?"

Peterson nodded and said, "Looks like I pulled you away from your work. I apologize for the intrusion, but I want to see Dave Harker. I've been over here half a dozen times the past few months and I've always been turned away. This time I aim to see him."

Peterson watched the foreman think about what he'd said. What would Garber do? Would the foreman turn him away again? Peterson noticed a few of the hands had stopped working and were watching them.

After a minute, Garber said, "Why don't you get down and wait on the porch, Mr. Peterson. I'll check on Dave. If he feels like talking to you, I let you in. If not, you'll just have to accept the fact that he's not up to visitors."

Peterson climbed the steps and sat down in a rocking chair. He glanced around the yard at the activity. The corral was full of horses. Several ranch hands were flitting this way and that. He was reminded that the Bar-N had looked and sounded like this not too long ago.

He was still watching the hands go about their chores when a woman joined him on the porch. Jeff was right. Dave did have someone caring for him. And they were also right that she was an attractive woman with a friendly smile.

She held out her hand. "I'm Lucy, Mr. Peterson. Dave said he'd love to visit with you. Come with me to the parlor. Hank will be along with Dave shortly."

Samuel took a seat in a soft chair and waited. He heard the creaking of the floor above him, then heard footsteps on the stairs. He turned and saw Dave slowly walking down the steps with Garber supporting him. Jeff had been right about this, too. Dave was not the Dave of old. He was pale, gaunt, and a mere shadow of the man he remembered from the past.

Peterson jumped up. "Here," he said. "Let me help you, Dave." He saw a grin appear on Dave's face.

"Sam. It's good of you to visit. It's been too long since we've had a chance to chew the fat. When Hank told me it was you, I had to get outta that damn bed if it killed me."

"It's been way too long, Dave."

It took them several minutes to get Dave situated in his chair. Peterson took a seat nearby where he could hear Dave's weak voice better. Lucy pulled up a chair and sat down beside Dave. Hank Garber stood at the doorway, leaning against the wall.

Samuel and Dave made small talk for several minutes: ranching, old times, and all the hardships they had endured over the years. Then there was a silence. Samuel knew now was the time for him say what he'd come to say.

"Dave," Peterson said. "What's going on at the Slant-H? We've been friends for going on thirty years. It was you who encouraged me to buy the Bar-N three years ago. Frankly, I don't understand what's happening. All your neighbors are struggling to make ends meet, and the Slant-H is overrun with cowhands and cattle. And you're buying out all those small ranchers around you who've given up and moved on. There's some talk that maybe all isn't as it appears to be around here. I don't believe for a minute that you're involved in anything illegal, but some of your other neighbors aren't so sure."

"You're referring to me," Garber said. "I hear the talk and see the stares when I go to town. You don't have to worry you're gonna hurt my feelings, Mr. Peterson. Say what's on your mind."

Peterson shrugged. "When you showed up at the ranch, Hank, things around here changed. Changed big. People simply don't understand. And all of us are losing cattle to the rustlers . . ."

"Except the Slant-H, you mean," Garber said, interrupting Peterson. "You're right. We've put a stop to it here on the Slant-H."

"For your information, we might've put an end to all of the rustling around here," Peterson said. He then told them about the gunfight at Hell's Holler. "The only thing is, one of them got away." Peterson noticed that Lucy stared at Garber the whole time he talked about the gunfight.

"You think it was me who got away?" Garber asked. "Go ahead, say it."

Dave Harker held up his hand and said, "Sam. I'd like for you to go out on the porch for a few minutes. Will you do that?"

Peterson looked at the three of them, then did as Dave asked without speaking. He sat in the rocking chair, confused by Dave's request. He realized the atmosphere was getting tense inside, so maybe Dave was trying to head off trouble.

Peterson heard the three of them talking in the parlor but couldn't make out the words. Whatever it was they were discussing involved all three of them. He could hear the woman's voice as well as Dave's and Garber's.

The screen door opened after several minutes. Lucy appeared, her face flushed, but with a smile. She ushered Peterson back into the parlor, where he took the same chair. This time Hank Garber sat on one side of Dave, and Lucy sat on the other side. All three had serious expressions on their faces.

"Sam," Dave said. "You've been a friend for a long time. I'll ask you to keep what we're about to tell you to yourself for the time being. Will you do that?"

Dave wanted to tell him something—with conditions tied to it. Samuel was eager to hear what Dave had to say, but there were limits to what he could hold secret.

"Of course, Dave," Peterson said. "Unless it's something my conscience won't allow. If you think that might be the case, then you'd better not tell me. You'd better just send me on my way."

Hank Garber leaned over and whispered something in Dave's ear. Dave nodded back at the foreman. "Hank says it's time to tell you. He'll do the talking since I'm afraid my stamina won't hold up."

Hank Garber then began talking.

CHAPTER SIXTY-TWO

Coy Dickson had the key in the padlock when Harlan Winters came up behind him.

"Coy," Winters said. "I know we've had our differences in the past, but you need to listen to me on this. We don't need any more killings around here, what with that marshal nosing around and all. I'll take them two young people out into the trees and hold 'em while you two finish your business inside the shaft. When you're finished, I'll bring 'em back and lock 'em up again. I can get one of the men over at the ranch to guard 'em for . . . say . . . three, four days, then turn 'em loose. We'll be long gone by then, and we won't have two more dead people on our hands. I wouldn't relish having that old Ranger and that marshal after us. I doubt we'd ever have another peaceful minute."

Dickson stared at Winters. The old man had a point worth considering. Dickson didn't want them on his trail either. He'd taken a certain amount of pride in the fact he'd never been caught by the law, but he'd always considered the odds before taking chances, too.

"You could be right," Dickson said, as he handed the key back to the one-armed man. "That old Ranger would make our lives hell from now on."

"I'll get one of the ranch hands to keep them under guard," Winters said. "I'll tell him not to turn them loose for three or four days."

Dickson motioned for Junior to join them. He explained what Harlan had suggested. The look on Junior's face told it all. He was relieved that two more deaths had been avoided. But little did Junior know what Dickson really had planned.

CHAPTER SIXTY-THREE

"I won't go back to the very beginning," Hank Garber said. "I'll just say that I rode with Nathan Bedford Forrest during the early months of the recent war. Then I rode with a couple more Confederate cavalry outfits after that. Some called us irregulars; some called us guerrillas. It was somewhere in Tennessee when the war ended for me. I never knew the name of the place. I was a sergeant riding with Colonel Abram Hicks when I was wounded in the upper thigh. It wasn't a bad wound, only bloody as hell. When the colonel rode up and saw me covered with blood, he turned and rode away, leaving me there at the mercy of the Yankees."

Garber stood and paced the parlor as he continued. He glanced at Lucy, who smiled and nodded for him to continue.

"The Yankees were right on Colonel Hicks' tail. I guess I couldn't fault him for leaving me like he did. Turns out it was a good break for me. The Yankees had a surgeon with them and he patched me up right good. The bad news was, I then bounced around from camp to camp until I landed at that hellhole, Camp Douglas in Illinois."

Garber turned to Sam Peterson. "I'm sure you know all about Camp Douglas, Mr. Peterson. It was a nightmare of disease, abuse, filth, and death. I got to Camp Douglas in late 'sixty-three. My wound had healed, but I was still weak from lack of rations, and from all the travel. The conditions at Camp Douglas didn't help. By the time I got to Douglas, I was sick of the war, sick of the killing, sick of everything. I never once thought I'd leave Douglas alive. There was no reason to think I would. Hundreds of men were dying every day all around me. The smell of the place is with me still.

"After being held in the camp several months, a Yankee major named Wilkinson showed up looking for prisoners of war to join a volunteer unit of the Union Army. He said the volunteers would be fighting the Indians out west. It meant changing uniforms, but it also meant putting Camp Douglas far behind me. And it meant getting away from the war. I thought about it long and hard, then signed up along with about two hundred other Rebels.

"I didn't want to use my real name. I knew it would shame my folks back home if they learned I'd put on a Yankee uniform—regardless of my reasons for doing so.

"Those of us who volunteered were assured we wouldn't be fighting soldiers in gray, but I didn't think that would make a difference to the folks at home if they knew. I grabbed the tag off a dead prisoner the guards were hauling off. His name happened to be Hank Garber. I put my tag on him—Clifford Harker."

Samuel Peterson sat there unable to talk. The man who had ridden into Carrsville and called himself Hank Garber was actually Dave Harker's son, Clifford. It all began to make sense to him as he thought about it. Clifford had returned to save the family ranch. And he had succeeded beyond all expectations.

"Yes, I'm really Cliff Harker, Mr. Peterson. I remember you riding by to visit Dad when you were with the Rangers." Garber pulled at his bushy beard. "That's why I chose to hide behind this sagebrush and rarely ride into Carrsville. The people around here have no idea I'm Dave's son, or that Lucy is my wife. I know what they think. They think I'm a thief who snuck in during the night and was trying to steal the Slant-H right out from under Pop."

"Why the mystery?" Samuel asked. "Why hide the fact you're Dave's son?"

Garber moved over and sat down beside Dave again. "I didn't know how my old friends would feel about me changing allegiance during the war. Especially Pop here. He was a Rebel through and through. I had a friend in Carrsville I could trust who kept me informed about the ranch and Dad's health. It got to the point I felt I had to return, regardless of the consequences. I couldn't bear to think of Pop not having family around when he needed me. Or the ranch going under after all these years."

Garber pointed to Lucy. "Lucy and I made the decision together."

Lucy then spoke: "I had understood Hank's dilemma long before we came to Carrsville. When I first met Hank, he owned a buggy and wagon shop in Tucson. He built handsome carriages with loving care and maintained a long waiting list for his handiwork. When we became aware of the situation in Carrsville, Texas, we sat down together and decided it would be best to come here to care for his father, and to take care of the family ranch. Hank sold his business to a competitor for a ridiculously high sum and we left Arizona behind us. That gave us enough money to do what had to be done here to keep the Slant-H running in the present, and to prepare it for the future."

She turned toward Hank and said. "But I never could persuade him to drop the masquerade. Until now."

Dave took hold of Lucy's arm. "She's been like a real daughter to me, Sam," he said. "Better than a daughter-in-law. The two of them told me right off who they were. Cliff had changed so much over the years that I didn't recognize him at first. But they didn't want me to think they were up to something shady, so Cliff explained why he had come home. I'll admit we had a long discussion about what he'd done, but we got it all cleared up. After a mess of questions and answers, both of us cried the rest of the week. When he told me about that Camp Douglas, I expect I would've done the same thing under those circumstances."

Sam Peterson shook his head in disbelief. "I don't know what to say. I'll keep it to myself as you asked. If you want my advice, Cliff, you'll tell everyone the truth and keep going on as you have been. It appears you and Lucy are going to be living here a long time. We'd be proud to have you as neighbors."

"Those are my sentiments, too," Lucy said. "The war is over. I'm sure there will be some who will hold onto the hate, but I think most people will understand once they get to know him again."

Samuel Peterson walked toward the door. "Dave," he said. "I'm glad you've got your family back with you. You get back on your feet and help them, you hear? They'll need you as much as you need them."

"I'll see that he does," Lucy said. "I can already see much improvement. I predict he'll be the same old Dave you remember in a few weeks."

CHAPTER SIXTY-FOUR

It was dark in the mine shaft when Sara heard the rattle of the padlock and chain. The door opened and a man handed her two tin plates of beans.

"Your meal," he said.

It wasn't the one-armed man who had caught her looking around.

"If you want to be helpful," she said, "how about giving me a key to that lock?"

"I do not think so," the guard said. Sara saw that he was a man with dark brown skin and long black hair. He even jangled a little when he walked with all his ornaments. She heard the rattle again as the lock and chain was replaced.

She began eating with her fingers. "They don't trust us with a knife and fork, huh?"

"I guess not. Basic beans, but they're not bad."

"If you like to eat beans with your fingers."

Sara and Jeff had been returned to the mine after spending three hours tied to a tree. The one-armed man had stayed with them the entire time, never talking, just watching. She had no idea why he had suddenly decided to let them have some fresh air. She doubted it was out of concern for their health. There was something else behind the tree episode.

She had found out what it was when they were unceremoniously shoved back into the dark mine shaft. The wooden door was standing wide open, and the small room had been cleaned out of the metal boxes and canvas bags.

"Dang it," Sara said when she saw it. "We're too late. They've taken the money and run."

After they had finished their meal, Sara paced around the dark shaft for a while, thinking about a way out of their ill-fated adventure. She dropped down beside Jeff and took his hand. She felt a soft squeeze and looked up at him. He kissed her and asked, "Did you think of a way out?"

"Maybe. What's the one thing that causes a man to do just about anything?"

He thought a minute, then said, "Money."

"Right. Money. Now take that guard out there. He's working because somebody pays him. Maybe he's being paid because he's a gunfighter or something. We don't know for sure. One thing we do know is that he's here at this mine watching over us because of the money."

"Go on."

"What if we offered him more money than he could earn in a year to let us go? Do you think he would take it?"

"Get serious, Sara. We don't have any money."

"Yeah, well, that's a problem all right. Still, we don't have anything to lose by trying, do we?" She rushed over to the iron bars and began shaking them. She hit on them with her fists, again and again. "Hey, guard," she yelled.

She heard footsteps, then, "Yes, *señorita.*"

"How would you like to earn five hundred dollars?"

She heard a soft laugh.

"Ah, *señorita,* I would love to earn five hundred dollars. My *señorita,* Elena, would love it, too. I must ask you. Do you have five hundred dollars?"

"I don't have it on me. But if you will help us escape, I'll get it for you, I promise. What is your name?"

"My friends call me Rio."

"I'm glad to meet you, Rio. My name is Sara. My friend and I are being held prisoner in this dark, dingy mine shaft for no good reason. We need to get out of here before those men do something bad to us. We have a friend named Mabry who will be looking for us. You don't want to be around when he shows up. He's a nasty man when he gets angry."

"Mabry, you say?"

"Yes. Frank Mabry. He's a real mean marshal. I'll see that you get the money if you'll let us go."

There was a long silence, then Rio spoke again. "Have a good night, *señorita.*"

"Dang it," she said.

CHAPTER SIXTY-FIVE

Sara had become accustomed to the dark of the mine shaft. She had no idea of the time, but knew it had to be close to midnight, if not later. How she knew that, she wasn't sure. It was just a feeling, more than anything. She hadn't slept any. She could hear Jeff's deep breathing and his occasional snore, otherwise there were few sounds.

Until she heard the rattle of the padlock and chain. The iron bars swung open and the guard who said his name was Rio was standing there. He had a finger to his lips in the "shush" sign. He motioned for her to wake up Jeff.

She went over to Jeff and shook him. "Wake up, Jeff," she whispered.

He opened his eyes. "What . . . what?"

"Be quiet," she said. "We're going to get out of here. No noise."

He jumped up, pulled on his boots, and then scrambled over to the entrance.

Rio whispered. "Quiet, *señorita*. I have horses waiting. We will ride away."

Sara thought of the five hundred dollars she had promised him. She didn't know where she would get it, but she was going to get it somehow.

Rio led them past the rear of the stone building and up the ridge. True to his word, there were three horses waiting, saddled and ready to ride.

"Quick," he said. "We must hurry. I do not think there is anyone around, but we must not take a chance."

They mounted the horses and walked them for several hundred yards.

"I think we are far enough away not to be heard," Rio said.

Sara and Jeff followed his lead, not speaking.

When they got near the Bar-N ranch house, Rio stopped them. "You go now. You are safe," he said.

Just as he was saying that, Sara heard horses running toward them.

"Quick," Rio said, as he reached for his rifle. "Over here in the trees." He led them into a thick stand of oak trees as the running horses got nearer. Sara saw Rio hold his rifle at the ready. The approaching riders then slowed their horses to a walk. Had they been seen? They were so close to getting away.

"Come on out, whoever you are," one of the men said. "I can see your silhouette. I don't want to shoot unless I have to."

Sara shouted, "Mabry. It's me, Sara. Don't shoot." She spurred her horse forward and almost collided with Moses.

"Sara," Mabry said. He turned in the saddle and saw Jeff, who was sitting alongside another man.

Captain Peterson rode up beside his daughter and said, "Little lady, we're going to have us a talk when we get back to the ranch. You'd better be thinking of some good answers."

"Mabry, this is Rio," Sara said, ignoring her father. "He saved our lives back at the silver mine."

"We'll talk about the silver mine later," Mabry said. He walked Moses over to Rio. "Thank you for what you did, Rio."

Rio smiled. "I remember you once did that for me, *señor*. Remember the man who was caught with his pants down? Rivero Vasquez? I am also called Rio by my friends."

Mabry laughed. "Rivero, is it? I guess no good deed goes unrewarded."

"What are you two talking about?" Sara asked. "Do you know him, Mabry?"

"I certainly do, but it's a long story and we don't have time for it now. I think we'd better start riding before anyone finds out you're gone. All three of you."

"I will leave you here," Rio said. "It was my pleasure to return a favor, *Señor* Mabry."

"No, Rio. You have to come with us," Sara said. "I'll find the money I promised you. You saved our lives."

Rio held up his hand. "I want no money. It would be an insult to take money for helping my friend, *Señor* Mabry. He saved my life, and now I have had a chance to repay. No money. Now you ride."

"Where will you go? You can't go back to the mine," Jeff said.

"I go to Mexico. I go home to see Elena. *Adios,* my friends," he said.

"One thing before you go, Rivero," Mabry said. "Who do you work for? Who sent you to the mine to guard them?"

"I do not know his name. I once heard a man call him Junior. That's all I know. I have been told to work, not ask questions. I think these are very bad men if they lock up a pretty young *señorita* in a mine shaft. I will work for them no more."

Rivero then slapped his horse and headed for the border.

"Junior," Peterson said. "That's the second time we've heard that name."

"It appears there is someone around here who is not who he seems to be," Mabry said. "And I think I know who he is."

CHAPTER SIXTY-SIX

The next morning, Mabry sat in the parlor listening to Jeff and Sara relate their experiences of the previous day. Mabry hadn't slept well that night, thinking of Sara and Jeff's close call. Neither of them realized how close they had come to death with Coy Dickson. The name Coy Dickson meant nothing to either of them. But Mabry knew.

Mabry had explained how he and Captain Peterson happened to run into them. He told them Sarge had ridden into Carrsville to find the captain at Hannah's insistence. Sarge had told Captain Peterson that Sara and Jeff had been gone overnight and couldn't be found. When Mabry and Peterson had learned Sara and Jeff were missing, they didn't hesitate. Mabry correctly guessed that Jeff had headed for Hell's Holler, since the lieutenant had been certain he'd seen a light through the trees. Then it was likely Sara had taken off after him when he failed to return.

Mabry said it was pure luck he and the captain hadn't missed them in the dark when they were returning to the ranch with Rivero Vasquez.

Sarge and Gil Alvarez had been waiting for them at the ranch, unsure if Mabry and Captain Peterson could find the two of them. If they hadn't returned to the ranch with Sara and Jeff by daylight, the two ex-Rangers had made up their minds to ride to the Slant-H ranch and have it out with Hank Garber and his men. They were certain Garber was behind all the trouble in the territory.

Mabry stood and stretched his limbs. He took a final sip of coffee and placed the cup on a table. "Let's go saddle our horses, Jeff. We've got some riding to do."

Mabry's first stop in Carrsville was the telegraph office. "I'm checking to see if you have you received any messages for Frank Mabry, or Lieutenant Julian Keener."

"Let me look," the counterman said, as he searched through several messages. "Yes. There's one for Keener, and two for Mabry."

Jeff reached for his message. "I'm Keener."

"Then you must be Mabry," the man said, handing Mabry his two messages.

The first one was from Colonel Floyd. Short and to the point.

Judgment correct. General Trowbridge Investigating.
Floyd

The second telegram was from Colonel Floyd, too. It had been sent several hours later and was longer and more detailed. Mabry was not surprised by its message.

"Anything important in your telegram?" Mabry asked.

"It was from Colonel Floyd. He said General Trowbridge has been asking a lot of questions in Washington and has learned a few interesting things. How would . . . Wait a minute. That's why you came to Carrsville after the gunfight, right? You put them on the trail of someone, didn't you?"

"It was a guess at the time. The proof showed up later."

"All the time I thought you were visiting your lady friend."

Mabry smiled at Jeff, then took a pad and scribbled out a message. He handed it across the counter to the operator. "Send this as addressed, please." He dropped six bits on the counter and said to Jeff. "Lieutenant Keener, we're going to clean up this mess once and for all."

"Have you figured out how you're going to do it?"

"Most of it. There's still a piece or two I haven't quite worked out yet." When they left the telegraph office, Mabry turned Moses toward the east.

"You want to tell me where we're going? I told you a long time ago, I don't do well with riddles."

"I thought you might've gotten better with them. You've improved in every other way since we first met in that Dallas hotel room."

Mabry smiled as he saw Jeff's face redden slightly beneath his sun-browned skin.

"All right," Jeff said. "I'll take a guess. There was something you found out at Hell's Holler that piqued your curiosity. You heard something that makes you believe we can find Coy Dickson out this direction."

"Close, but not totally correct. Think a little harder."

They rode for a quarter of a mile, then Jeff snapped his fingers. "Last night after Rio let us out of the mine he told you he worked for a man called Junior. You know who that man is, don't you?"

Mabry grinned. "See. You've improved in that area, too."

"I still haven't worked it all out yet," Jeff said. "Aren't you going to tell me?"

Mabry spurred Moses and took off at a gallop. "You'll find out in less than an hour. Let's ride."

The ranch house and surrounding yard of the Whipsaw ranch was quiet and peaceful as Mabry stopped to scan the area. He didn't want to ride into an ambush, even though he thought it highly unlikely. Mabry couldn't see activity anywhere around the dwelling, or the barns. The place appeared to be deserted.

"Something's not right here, Jeff," Mabry said. He clicked his tongue at Moses and urged him forward, his hand hovering over his Colt as he continued to scan his surroundings. When he reached the front of the house, he saw the front door open. He saw something else, too. Mabry jumped off Moses and hurried up the steps, Jeff right behind him.

Hugh Fowler was stretched out on his back over a pool of blood. Mabry bent over him and determined he had been dead for several hours. He saw at least one gunshot to the chest and another gunshot to the head. Behind Fowler, he saw the body of a second man. He stepped over Fowler and found the other man lying on his stomach, also in a pool of blood. Mabry kneeled down and found him to be dead, too.

"Jeff. Here's your one-armed man."

Jeff stepped closer and got a better look at Fowler. "Was this the man Rio had mentioned? The one called Junior?"

Mabry nodded. "Hugh Fowler, Jr."

"How did you know it was Fowler?"

Mabry looked around the room and found Fowler's copy of the novel *Ben-Hur*. He opened it to the inscription page and handed Jeff the open book. "Read this."

Best Wishes to Hugh Fowler, Jr.
An old friend and colleague.
Lew Wallace

Jeff sat down in a chair on the porch. He pointed at the body of Fowler and asked. "Was Fowler part of the rustling ring, or the train robbery?"

"Maybe both. The train robbery, for sure. He and that one-armed man had hid the money at the mine and were waiting until things calmed down before spending the spoils. We'll have to get the details from Colonel Floyd. I suspect Fowler had a job in the Washington area that gave him access to the information about currency transfers. I'd bet my boots that Fowler and another well-placed government man devised a plan to steal the money and needed someone like Dickson to do the dirty work."

Mabry made a gesture toward Fowler's body. "Asking Dickson to help him wasn't a smart thing to do. I imagine Coy Dickson and his gang did the actual robbery and killing. Dickson then killed Fowler and the one-armed man and took off with all the money. Remember Dickson's trademark: leave no witnesses."

Jeff shook his head again. "That's one cold-blooded killer. I guess we were all wrong about Hank Garber being behind the robbery and rustling."

CHAPTER SIXTY-SEVEN

Coy Dickson had decided to go for it all. Junior and Harlan Winters had been all that stood in his way to more riches than he could imagine. They had been easily handled; an old one-armed man and a soft gentleman rancher. Now his only challenge was how to get out of the territory with the money. It had turned out to be a more difficult problem than he'd anticipated. The remaining gold coins were packed in thick, weighty canvas bags, and the greenbacks were packed in bulky metal boxes. He marveled at how Junior and Harlan had managed to store all of them in that one small room at the mine.

After he had forced them to haul the money back to the ranch, he no longer needed them. He could still see the surprised look on their faces when he pulled out his revolver and pointed it at them. He had shot Winters first, then Junior.

Then he had to deal with how to handle the money. Carrying it on a horse with him was out of the question. The money was too bulky and too heavy. A packhorse—maybe two, possibly even three. A wagon would be the obvious answer, but that presented too many problems. With a loaded wagon, he'd have to stick to the established roads and known trails. That wouldn't be wise with the law after him. And a wagon would be too slow. Dickson knew he needed to get out of the territory fast. A wagon wouldn't allow him to do that.

Another option he considered was to not do anything. Find an out-of-the-way place and hunker down until the law gave up looking for him. He'd done just that more than once in the past with great results. By now Junior Fowler and Harlan Winters had probably been found at the ranch, as well as the two people at the mine. The law would be out in force searching for him. They might even bring in troops to help, since dead soldiers were involved. Maybe that was the smart thing for him to do—wait 'em out. But where?

That old line shack? Or, even better, that gal's place he frequented over near Red Mesa. He could get there with two packhorses, or even a wagon, in one night's travel easy. That's what he'd do. He'd hole up at Delia's place until things quieted down.

He had eluded the law for over fifteen years. Ever since that first bank holdup in Missouri. He could dodge 'em for another fifteen years if need be. He just had to outguess 'em. He'd always outsmarted those who tried to catch him. He didn't see this situation as being any different.

CHAPTER SIXTY-EIGHT

It had turned out to be a long day for Frank Mabry. Longer than he'd expected. Jeff had ridden back to Carrsville to get Sheriff Tolliver while Mabry searched through Fowler's house. There was little to be found that Mabry took to be helpful.

When Tolliver arrived with one of his deputies, Mabry and Jeff headed back toward the Bar-N. Both were weary and ready to bring this whole messy affair to an end. Thus far they had determined the name of the soldiers' killer, and had located the stolen money—in a general sense. As an aside, they had also helped put an end to a rustling ring that had run rampant around the territory.

When they got to the cutoff in the road that led them to the Bar-N, Mabry said, "You go on to the ranch, Jeff. I think I'll stop by and visit with a friend. I'll be back at the ranch tomorrow, and then we'll see what we can do about this Dickson feller and the money."

Jeff grinned. "You get in at a respectable hour, you hear?"

The Long Horn was quieter than normal when he pushed through the doors. There were several men in the place. The smoke and smell were the same as before, but the atmosphere seemed more subdued. He liked what he saw—and heard. Even the piano player was playing a softer tune. Maybe Fanny had taken the first steps to clean up the place.

Louie spotted him and cocked his head toward the office.

Mabry nodded his thanks.

To be polite, Mabry knocked on the door.

"Come on in, it's unlocked."

Fanny was standing beside her desk holding a coal oil lantern. When she saw him, she yelped like a puppy. "Mabry. You're just in time. Help me get this lantern on the hanger. I can't reach it."

He took the lantern from her and placed it on its hanger.

"I've been scrubbing and cleaning all day," she said. "Can't you tell it's brighter in here now?"

"Yep, it's much brighter. And the saloon is brighter, too—and quieter."

"Thanks to you," she said, as she got on her tiptoes and kissed him. "You going to be around for a while, or just dropping in to say goodbye."

He shrugged. "Which would you prefer?"

"Huh," she grunted. "You know my answer. I'd never let you just drop in to say goodbye. I'd rope you and hog-tie you to keep you here if I could."

Mabry laughed. "I'll admit, I've never had a female try that on me. It might turn out to be mighty interesting."

Fanny took him by the arm and pushed him toward the door. "Come on. This place is so quiet now, I could use some real excitement."

Mabry followed her up the stairs to the blue door with a grin plastered on his face.

CHAPTER SIXTY-NINE

Two full days had passed since the Bar-N gunfight, as the people around Carrsville had begun to call it. The town was still in shock to find out one of their finest citizens, Hugh Fowler, had tried to enrich himself by robbing a train. But they were equally pleased that the hooligans who had cluttered up their town for so long had been run out.

Mabry had ridden all around the countryside north of Carrsville searching for any sign of Coy Dickson. He had bought drinks at every crossroads joint and had pumped and pried every person he could find. Dickson had seemingly dropped off the planet. Being a man of positive nature, he took this to mean that Dickson had gone into hiding to wait out the storm. Hauling around whatever was left of five hundred thousand dollars in coins and greenbacks would not be an easy chore.

At every stop, he left a copy of Sheriff Tolliver's wanted poster with the same request, "If you know where Dickson is, it'll be worth a thousand dollars to you if either the sheriff or I find him there."

Then he would drop a few of Colonel Floyd's coins on the table and say, "Drink up boys and keep your eyes and ears open."

He estimated he had ridden two hundred miles as he crisscrossed the area searching for any clue of Dickson's location. A few of the men he questioned clammed up and wouldn't talk to him. He heard the term "damned law" thrown at his back more than a few times.

Jeff had been doing the same thing to the south of Carrsville. He'd had no better luck in finding Dickson than Mabry had. "All we've got left on our plate is to find Coy Dickson, right?" Jeff asked.

"Yep. And what's left of half a million dollars."

Mabry had returned to the Bar-N after a hard day in the saddle on the third day of his search for Dickson. He took Moses to the barn, rubbed him down, and gave him an ample helping of grain. He stretched his sore muscles, then walked up to the porch, where he got a surprise. Sitting in one of the rockers beside Samuel Peterson was Dave Harker. His face had filled out some since he had seen him at the ranch, his color was much improved, and he looked to be in good spirits.

Mabry nodded. "Mr. Harker. It's good to see you out and about. Did you make the trip by yourself?"

"No. My daughter-in-law, Lucy, is making the rounds and introducing herself. She said it's the neighborly thing to do."

Mabry gave Captain Peterson a big grin.

Dave caught the look and laughed. "You guessed this a while back, didn't you, Marshal? Tell him the whole story, Samuel."

Peterson then told Mabry all about Hank Garber and the circumstances that led him to hide his real identity. "Hank is making a circuit of the ranches doing the same thing Lucy is doing here," Peterson said. "That, plus us putting an end to that gang of rustlers ought to quieten down all the rumors about the Slant-H."

"I can't really blame them for what they were thinking," Dave said. "I expect Hank . . . er . . . Cliff . . . and I handled it wrong from the start. Looking back, we should've come right out and let everyone know who he was." Dave nodded toward the doorway. "Lucy tried her best to get us to do that. But the

Harker family always had this stubborn streak. We always thought we knew best."

Peterson said, "There's a peaceful feeling in the air at last, Dave. And it's a good feeling. I have an idea our best years are still ahead of us."

CHAPTER SEVENTY

Washington City

General Alfred Trowbridge tapped on the door of the Secretary of War's office. Alongside him were Major Lucius Lederer and Colonel Everett Edmundson.

"Enter."

Secretary Martin Greenwell sat behind a wide mahogany desk with a pen in his hand as the three officers entered. He took off his eyeglasses and rubbed the bridge of his nose as he motioned them to take a seat.

Trowbridge thought that Greenwell had a weary, tired look about him. He also wondered if Greenwell had any inkling of why they had requested the meeting.

"Mr. Secretary," Trowbridge said, nodding his head toward his fellow officers. "I believe you've met Major Lederer and Colonel Edmundson?"

"I have. Now, what's this urgent business you have to discuss with me, General?"

"Major Lederer and Colonel Edmundson have been investigating the Colorado currency robbery, sir. And the murder of the three soldiers."

Secretary Greenwell continued to toy with his eyeglasses, and cleaned them with a white cloth while General Trowbridge was speaking, not looking at the general. After a moment, Greenwell looked up and said, "I understand there has been a break in the case in Texas. But I fail to understand what that has got to do with you gentlemen here in Washington."

"Mr. Secretary, the deputy marshal who was assigned to the case contacted Colonel Otis Floyd with questions he wanted answered. Floyd in turn contacted me with those questions. I assigned these two officers to find the answers."

"Yes, yes, get on with it, General. Get to your point."

"The answers led us straight to your office, Mr. Secretary."

Secretary Greenwell's head jerked up and his hands stopped fiddling with his eyeglasses. He looked at each of the officers, then returned to glare at General Trowbridge. "You had better explain yourself, General. And I should caution you that unwarranted accusations will not be tolerated by this office. Is that understood?"

"Yes, sir."

"Then continue—with care."

General Trowbridge spoke with the full confidence that he knew what had transpired and was not intimidated at all by the secretary's threats. "Sir, the whole bloody Colorado incident was conceived, planned, and executed by your good friend and advisor, Hiram McDougal."

"Hiram?" Greenwell asked. "That's quite a statement, General. Are you able to back it up with more than talk or supposition? Again, I advise you to be cautious with your accusations."

"We are quite certain, sir," Colonel Edmundson said. "We're on our way to arrest Mr. McDougal now. He and another man were the planners and brains behind the theft of five hundred thousand dollars. Furthermore, they were indirectly responsible for the deaths of the three soldiers . . ."

"And several other deaths that occurred in Texas," Trowbridge added.

"You said Hiram and another man, General?"

"Yes. Hugh Fowler. I believe he had been another of your

close associates over the years."

Greenwell lowered his head and said, "Yes. I have known Hugh Fowler for many years. A good man. It's hard to think . . ."

"Fowler was killed by the very man he and McDougal brought into this affair to do their dirty work," Trowbridge said. "Just reward, I would venture to say." Trowbridge stood. "Since this unfortunate and deadly affair began at your doorstep, Mr. Secretary, and the man responsible was under your oversight, we thought it proper to advise you before arresting Mr. Mc-Dougal. Our investigation will continue on orders from the president."

Trowbridge could see that Secretary Greenwell was shaken. He was perspiring and he had begun to stammer as he spoke. "You . . . you . . . don't think that I . . . ?"

"All I can say at this time, Mr. Secretary, is that we are continuing to investigate. I fully expect that you will be seeing us again at some point in the near future. Now, if you will excuse us, we must see to our business with Mr. McDougal."

Greenwell raised his hands to his face, and hid behind them. "Hiram, you damned greedy Scotsman. What have you done to me?"

CHAPTER SEVENTY-ONE

Four days had passed with no sign of Coy Dickson. Mabry had come to believe the killer had slipped away somehow. Dickson had a reputation of being a slippery fox. He'd often been heard to brag about never being caught by the law. Mabry and Jeff had discussed their situation, and both had concluded they had given it all they had to give. They could take some consolation in the fact that of all those involved, only one had gotten away.

The flaw with that reasoning was the one man who had gotten away took the money with him. And had gotten away with the murders of at least five people. Bannister had sent Mabry a telegram for him to call off the hunt. So the decision had been taken out of his hands. Colonel Floyd had likewise sent Lieutenant Keener a similar message.

It was close to noontime when the issue had come to an end as far as Mabry was concerned. He would leave for the Double-M ranch the following morning to help Woody for a few days. Jeff was told to meet Colonel Floyd at nearby Fort Nelson for their return trip to Washington.

Mabry saddled Moses and led him to the front of the house. "I'm going to Carrsville to say goodbye to a friend," Mabry told Jeff. "You and Sara had better get yourselves straightened out before you leave, too."

Jeff's face reddened. "I guess we'd better do that. I'm not leaving until tomorrow, so I'll see you before I go."

★　★　★　★　★

When Mabry walked into the Long Horn Saloon, he had to look twice to make sure he hadn't entered the wrong building. The inside of the saloon had been painted a bright red color. Purple draperies had been added to the two large windows, and the floor had been swept, mopped, and polished. And the smell. Mabry couldn't believe the difference. The saloon smelled like a pine forest.

He stepped in and unconsciously wiped his boots on a thick rug near the doorway. He looked up and noticed Louie, who had a wide grin spread across his face. Mabry grinned back at him.

"I thought I was in the wrong place," Mabry said.

Louie motioned him over and whispered. "Fanny has been working our asses off cleaning and painting. It seems to be paying off. We've had to put on a second bartender to handle the evening crowds. She even hired a swamper to keep the place clean."

"Good for her."

"She's in the office. I don't guess you have to knock anymore."

But he did.

"Come on in. It's unlocked."

Fanny was seated behind her desk writing in a journal. When she looked up, she smiled. "Mabry, your bright idea about cleaning up this place has about killed me. I don't ever want to see another mop or paintbrush."

"You've got a first class place now, Fanny. As good as any I've seen. And I've seen quite a few in my day."

She walked around the desk and threw her arms around his neck. "Thanks for the suggestion." She kissed him, then backed away. "I'll ask you again. Are you going to be here for a while, or just passing through?"

Before he could answer, Louie hurried through the office

doorway. "Sorry to interrupt, but I thought the marshal needed to see this." He held out his hand, palm up. It was a shiny gold coin. "A cowpoke just bought a bottle of whiskey with it."

Mabry rushed to the door and scanned the room. He didn't see anyone who looked like Coy Dickson. He called the bartender over. "Point him out."

"That's him. The one over there sitting by the window."

"Thanks," Mabry said, as he headed for the table.

The man was older than Dickson by several years. He had a broad red face with a drooping mustache. His clothes suggested that he was a cowpuncher.

"Mind if I join you?" Mabry asked, then sat down before the man could object.

The man stared at Mabry's badge. "I don't usually drink with a marshal." He lifted his glass and held it out toward Mabry. "This is a real honor, Marshal. Can I pour you one before it's all gone?"

"No, thanks. I need to know one thing, then I'll leave you to your drinking." Mabry spun the gold coin on the table. "How did you come by this gold coin?"

"I didn't steal it, if that's what you're thinking. I won it in a poker game over at Red Mesa." He held up his hand. "That's the truth, Marshal. This cowpoke musta lost twenty of 'em that day. He'd lose a hand, then reach into his pocket and bring out more of 'em. He shore enough does like his poker playing."

"Red Mesa you say?"

"That's what I said. The Live Oak Saloon. There's just three or four buildings in Red Mesa, so you can't miss it if it's your intention to go there."

"You see this poker player there more than once?"

"He came in two days ago, then kept coming back. Like I said, he shore does like to play poker."

"Do you know where he hangs his hat at night?"

"You're asking a lot of questions, Marshal. Is this man wanted for something? Am I about to get somebody hung?"

Mabry flipped the gold coin to the man. "Tell me where he holes up. If I catch him where you say, you're going to be one thousand dollars richer with the reward. I wouldn't leave town until I knew for sure, if I were you."

CHAPTER SEVENTY-TWO

Red Mesa was a two hour ride from Carrsville according to Fanny. If the information the cowpoke had given him held up, Mabry should find Dickson at a cabin located in a grove of trees near a fork in the road. The cowpoke, whose name was Owens, said the two of them had spent a night of poker playing and drinking. The man had gotten so drunk, Owens had to haul him out of the saloon and back to his cabin. When Mabry showed Owens the wanted poster, the cowpoke nodded his head and said, "That's him. That's Arkansas, or that's what he called hisself, anyway."

When he judged he was half a mile from the fork in the road Owens had described, Mabry pulled Moses off the road. He traveled through the thick scrub brush and prickly pear. It was slow going. Mabry tried to stay parallel to the road, but often got sidetracked because of the thick brush. As he neared the fork, he dismounted and threaded his way through the thorny bushes where he could get a better view of the cabin. He found the small cabin in the fork like Owens had said. It looked to be a simple cabin in all respects; one room made of rough-cut logs with a crude stone chimney running up a side wall. A thin spiral of smoke drifted upwards from the chimney.

Mabry could see a door in front with a small window on each side. There was a saddled horse tied to a bush in front of the cabin, and two more hobbled horses near the trees. Mabry sat back, trying to decide what to do next. Then the cabin door

253

opened. A man appeared. It was Coy Dickson, all right. He was peeling an apple with a small knife and dropping the peelings on the ground. Dickson sliced off a hunk of the apple, put it in his mouth, and wiped the knife on his shirt. Dickson looked around for a few minutes, then went back inside the cabin.

Mabry considered what he could do now that he'd found him. Owens said the man was holed up with a woman at the cabin. Mabry didn't want the woman to get caught in a crossfire, but how was he going to keep her away from it? He checked his Colt and rolled the cylinder. He gave out with a sigh, then bent low and crept around the bushes until he was far to the left of the house. The cabin sat within the fork of the stage road, so he had to cross over at some point. He continued on until he was out of sight of the windows and the door should it open again. Staying low, he ran across the road and dropped down in a shallow ditch. No sounds came from the cabin. Dickson hadn't seen him.

Mabry tried to relax and calm himself. He took a deep breath and let it out slowly. He was now in position to slip up to the windowless side of the house without being seen. Mabry lay still and listened. He was convinced Dickson hadn't spotted him, so he raced toward the cabin. When he reached the chimney, he heard loud talking and laughter coming from inside. Apparently Dickson was not too worried about anyone finding him.

Mabry moved to the back of the house to see if there was a rear door. He saw the cabin had a back door that sagged on rotten leather straps. He knew then how he was going to take Dickson.

He eased up to the front corner of the shack and took another deep breath. "Dickson," he shouted. "This is Marshal Frank Mabry. Come on out, it's all over. Throw out your gun and walk out."

There was a moment of silence, then, "I ain't coming out,

Mabry. You come in and get me if you've got the nerve. I ain't got nothing to lose. I done killed too many of them soldiers. If I kill you, it ain't going make no difference. They can't hang me more'n once."

"Send your lady friend out, and I'll oblige you. I wouldn't want her to get hurt in the crossfire."

"First of all, she ain't no lady, and second of all, I don't care if she gets caught in a crossfire or not. How'd you find me, Mabry?"

"The same way you led me to Carrsville. You like to spread those gold coins around too much. Your daddy shoulda told you gambling was the devil's work."

"Quit preaching and come get me. We'll see who meets the devil first."

"Lady," Mabry shouted. "You get yourself down flat on the floor. I'm going to be bursting through that door any minute. And when I do, I'll be shooting at anything I see."

Mabry then ran around to the back of the cabin. He had his gun in hand as he took two running steps, threw his left shoulder into the rear door, and burst into the cabin. Mabry saw the surprised look on Dickson's face, just before he put two bullets into the killer's chest.

Mabry hurried over to him. He was dead, no doubt. He looked over at the woman who was cowering in the corner. "Are you hurt, ma'am?"

The woman shook her head.

Just to be on the safe side, he gathered up all the weapons he could find in the cabin. Mabry didn't want an angry lover trying to get revenge on him when he wasn't looking.

He dragged Dickson out the front door where the killer's black stallion was tied. He threw Dickson's body over the saddle and tied him down. Then he returned to the cabin. At the back of the cabin he saw a pile of boxes covered with a ratty blanket.

He gave the blanket a jerk and found the canvas bags and the metal boxes.

It took him the better part of an hour to get the currency loaded on the two packhorses. Relief swept over him as he pointed Moses toward Carrsville. He'd turn Dickson's body over to Sheriff Tolliver, making sure the sheriff knew it was the cowpoke Owens who had provided the information. Then he'd take the stolen currency to Lieutenant Keener and let him handle it from there.

CHAPTER SEVENTY-THREE

Two days after Coy Dickson and the money had been found, Mabry sat on the porch of the Bar-N ranch house with Samuel Peterson and Colonel Otis Floyd. Colonel Floyd had accompanied a detachment of troopers who had arrived the previous night and made camp behind the barn. Floyd had sent orders for Jeff to remain at the ranch with the currency until the troopers from Fort Nelson arrived to serve as an escort back to the fort. In the meantime, Jeff and Sara had counted four hundred and sixteen thousand dollars in recovered currency.

"General Trowbridge says all hell is breaking loose in Washington," Colonel Floyd said with a laugh. "Secretary Greenwell is fighting for his job."

"Was Greenwell involved in any way?" Peterson asked.

"I can't say for sure. If he was involved, Trowbridge will dig it out." Floyd jerked a thumb over at Mabry. "Trowbridge is a lot like this fellow. He won't call it quits until he gets what he's after."

Floyd went on to explain that both Hugh Fowler and Hiram McDougal had been longtime friends of the secretary. When Mabry sent Floyd the telegram asking him to check on Fowler's connections in Washington, McDougal's name was on top of the list, followed closely by that of Secretary Greenwell.

"McDougal had all the information he needed to carry out the robbery," Floyd said. "Schedules, routes, everything. Including knowledge that Captain Quint Rainey had been told about the coins showing up in Carrsville. They might've gotten by with the whole thing if Dickson hadn't killed those soldiers. I have a sneaking suspicion McDougal saw this as a way to discredit Greenwell and possibly be named Secretary of War himself."

"Was it McDougal who had Rainey killed?" Peterson asked.

Floyd shrugged. "We're still learning the details. When Hiram McDougal found out Hugh Fowler had been killed, he began playing the politician and blaming everything on Fowler. McDougal said Fowler had Harlan Winters kill Rainey, and thought Rainey's death would stop the investigation."

"It almost had to be by McDougal's orders," Mabry said. "McDougal was the one man who knew Rainey was investigating the robbery."

Floyd nodded. "And I feel certain McDougal, or Fowler, would've had Winters kill you and Lieutenant Keener, too, if he'd known you would end up in Carrsville."

"Rainey kept his information about Carrsville a secret I guess," Mabry said. "McDougal and Fowler never figured on us finding that little piece of bloody paper in Rainey's pocket pointing us toward Carrsville."

Colonel Floyd stood and extended his hand to Mabry. "Thanks for bringing this to a satisfactory conclusion, Marshal." He turned to Captain Peterson and shook his hand as well. "And you, Mr. Peterson, for your hospitality. We must get on the road if we're to reach Fort Nelson before dark."

"Good luck getting Lieutenant Keener away from here, Colonel," Peterson said. "I think he's taken a liking to the West."

Floyd laughed. "He doesn't know it yet, Mr. Peterson, but you might be seeing more of that young man in the near future. Maybe more than you might like."

★ ★ ★ ★ ★

Jeff and Sara had put Jeff's free time over the past two days to good use. The two of them had strolled over much of the ranch, and had ridden around the rest of it. Jeff sensed that Hannah and Samuel seemed pleased at the unexpected development between the two of them.

"I hate for you to go," Sara said. "I don't know what I'm going to do around here without you. I've kinda got used to you being here."

"Oh, maybe another greenhorn will drop by someday and you can make fun of him for entertainment."

She punched him in the ribs. "You're not a greenhorn anymore. I'm not so sure you ever were. An ole Easterner, yes. But a greenhorn, no."

"Maybe, just maybe, I'll be seeing you again before too long."

She dropped his hand, took him by the shoulders, and turned him around to face her. "What do you mean? Tell me. Now."

He smiled. "Well, it seems I'm a kind of a hero around the War Department now. The way I told the story, I recovered the money, and caught the thieves. All by myself."

"You did no such thing," she said. Then she asked, "You didn't really tell them that, did you?"

"No," he said, laughing at her sincerity. "But I might as well have, the way Colonel Floyd has been acting. He's talking a promotion and an assignment to wherever I want to go."

"And?" she asked. "Go on, go on."

"I've asked for Fort Nelson. There's some things about this country that have grown on me. The dust, the wind, and maybe another thing or two. I don't know yet how it will turn out."

"Yee-iii!" Sara shouted. She grabbed him around the neck and kissed him. "Good choice, Lieutenant Keener."

"I'll write you as soon as I know anything definite. Now I have to run. They're calling for me."

He gave her one last kiss and ran toward the waiting cavalry. Sergeant Stankowski had his troops mounted and ready to ride. A canvas-covered army ambulance had been brought to transport the currency to Fort Nelson.

Before he climbed in, Jeff grabbed Mabry's hand. "Thanks for putting up with me, Deputy Marshal Mabry. It was a memorable month for sure. One I'll never forget. Maybe we'll see each other again sometime."

"I hope so. Good luck, kid," Mabry said with a grin.

Reed Bannister will be proud of how I met this challenge.

After the caravan had departed, Mabry shook hands with all the ex-Rangers. He hugged Hannah and Sara, then climbed aboard Moses. He spurred Moses and took off down the road. As he did, he turned back toward them and shouted something.

"What did he say?" Sara asked.

"Beats me," Sarge said. "Sounded something like 'blue door.' "

ABOUT THE AUTHOR

Ben Tyler, a graduate of Murray State University, is a former secondary school teacher, and human resources manager in the chemical industry. He is an avid golfer (of the hacker variety) when time permits. He currently lives in Western Kentucky near Kentucky and Barkley lakes. His previous novel was *Echoes of Massacre Canyon*.